Author dedication: To Eva, For Mockingbirds,
Empires, Handmaids and more

Monstrum House: Taken Over
published in 2010 by
Hardie Grant Egmont
85 High Street
Prahran, Victoria 3181, Australia
www.hardiegrantegmont.com.au

A CiP record for this title is available from the National Library of Australia.

Text copyright © 2010 Zana Fraillon
Illustration and design copyright © 2010 Hardie Grant Egmont

Design and illustration by Simon Swingler
Typeset by Ektavo

Printed in Australia by McPherson's Printing Group

1 3 5 7 9 10 8 6 4 2

Taken Over

By Zana Fraillon

Illustrations by Simon Swingler

hardie grant EGMONT

It was a stupid thing to do. A very, *very* stupid thing to do. Jasper McPhee wished he hadn't done it. He wished he hadn't even *thought* about doing it. But he had. The stupid thought had scuttled into his head, and before he had a chance to shoo it back out, he had done it. And now he was in serious trouble.

'You are so dead,' Felix whispered.

Jasper was hiding under a table in the food hall. It was the first day of his second year at the Monstrum House School for Troubled Children, and he was already in trouble.

He was trying to avoid Bruno, the head prefect.

'Do you think he'll remember?' Jasper asked Felix hopefully. 'He could have forgotten. After all, we were away for a whole six weeks. Lots of stuff can happen over the holidays.'

But Jasper knew Bruno would never forget what he'd done at the end of last year. 'Why did I do it?' he groaned.

Saffy snorted. 'Because you are a complete –'

Jasper jabbed Saffy in the shins before she could finish the sentence.

Jasper peered out at the prefects from under the table. Bruno was the only one he recognised from the previous year. The rest were new. Jasper couldn't believe it. Bruno had had it in for him all of first year. He had personally given Jasper more penalty points than all the other prefects put together. Which is why, on Bruno's last day, Jasper had given him a little going-away present.

'I thought the prefects only did one year here,' whispered Jasper. 'They're not meant to come back!'

'Well, it looks like he did. Maybe he had some unfinished business?' said Saffy.

Jasper softly thumped his head against the table leg. 'Kill me now and get it over with,' he mumbled to himself. He *knew* Bruno wouldn't let him off the hook easily.

Jasper thought of the way the rotten eggs had sailed perfectly through the open windows of the prefects' bus. He thought of the look on Bruno's face when the eggs hit him. Bruno had looked out the window and his eyes had met Jasper's. His face had been dripping with stinking, disgusting, rotten egg. And Jasper had waved as the bus pulled away.

It had been pretty awesome. In fact, better than awesome. It had been pure *genius*.

Except now, Bruno was back. Now, it didn't seem so genius. Now it just seemed stupid.

'Hang on,' Felix muttered quietly. 'I don't think it's him.'

Jasper rolled his eyes. 'Very funny. Of course it's him! I know the thug brigade all look like the same lumps of muscle, but that's definitely ...' Jasper stopped talking. Bruno was carefully surveying the students in the food hall. There *was* something different.

'Yeah,' Saffy murmured. 'There's no scar.'

Jasper squinted at the prefect. Saffy was right. Bruno had a huge scar running down his face, but this prefect didn't.

'And I think his eyes are a bit closer together,' Felix commented.

'So, d'you think it's safe to come out?' Jasper whispered.

'Yeah, sure,' Saffy said. 'It's definitely not him.'

Jasper took a deep breath and crawled out from under the table and up onto his seat. But as soon as he did, the prefect's eyes locked onto him.

Jasper held his breath.

The prefect reached into his pocket and pulled out a photo.

'Uh, Jasper. I think he's seen you,' said Felix.

'Maybe you should get back under the table,' Saffy suggested.

'Too late,' Jasper whispered. The prefect was heading their way.

Jasper leapt up from the table and ran. There was no way he was hanging around to get beaten up by a Bruno look-alike. Jasper was a fast runner. He could outrun most kids.

And even with all the junk food he'd gorged on over the holidays, he was still speedy. The door was only two steps away …

Jasper made a dive for it, but he was wrenched back by the hood of his jumper. He felt himself lifted up and spun slowly around. The Bruno look-alike held Jasper at least a foot off the ground. He pressed his nose against Jasper's. 'You're McPhee, aren't you?'

Jasper gulped, 'Um, well,' he began. Being suspended in the air by a hoodie was really quite uncomfortable.

The prefect dropped Jasper to the ground. 'My brother told me *all* about you,' he sneered, and shoved Jasper out of the food hall and into the corridor, where they were alone. No-one could help him now.

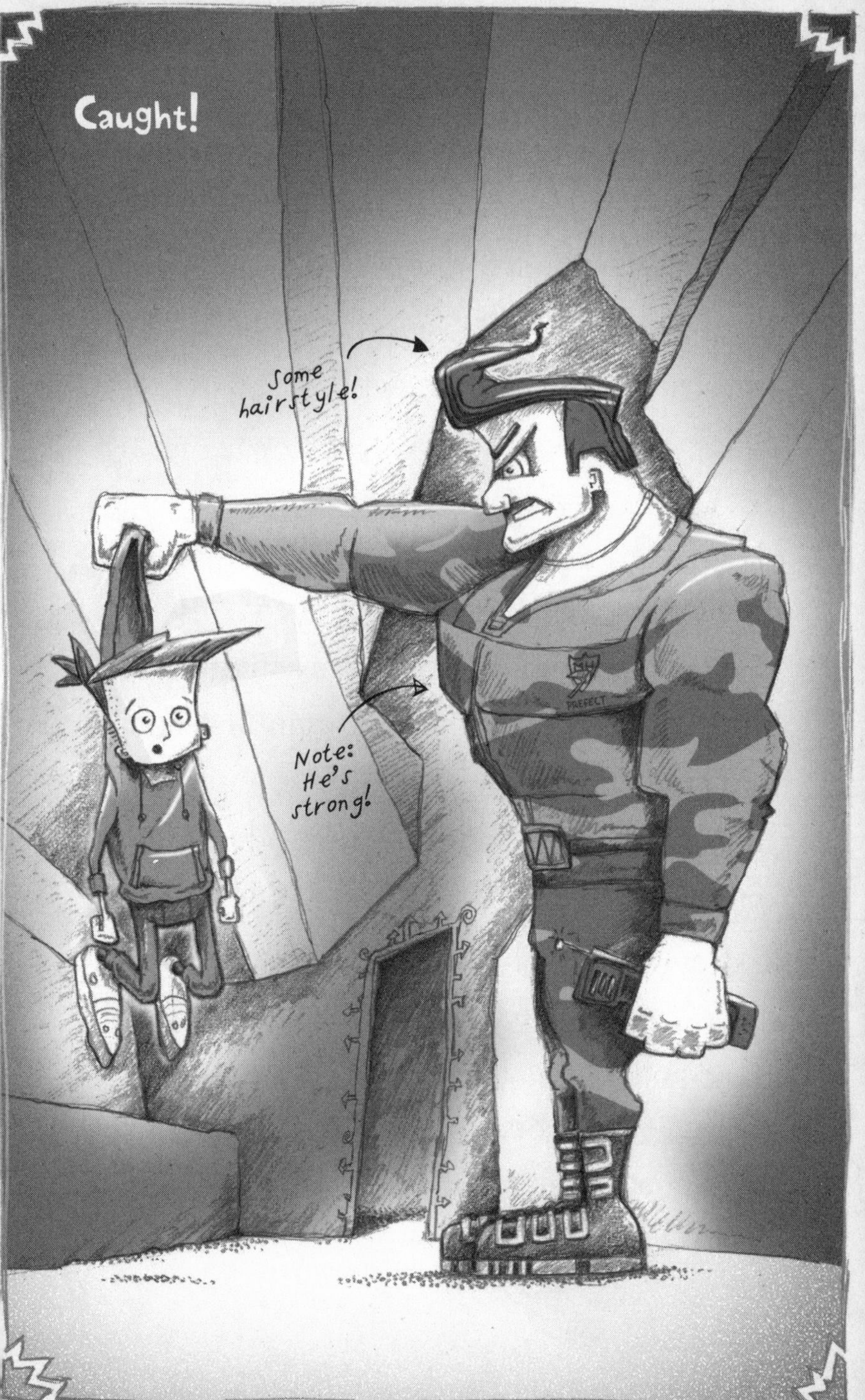
Caught!
Some hairstyle!
Note: He's strong!
PREFECT

Jasper closed his eyes. *Bruno's brother!* He was going to die. And if this guy was anything like Bruno, it would be a long and painful death.

Jasper hated the prefects at Monstrum House. They were probably the worst thing at this place, which was saying a lot. The monsters were dangerous, the teachers were definitely creepy, but the prefects were just nasty.

Jasper had been to plenty of schools. He'd been expelled countless times. But he'd never been to a school like this – with prefects who wanted to beat you up, teachers who could read your thoughts, and monsters all over the place. But perhaps the weirdest thing about Monstrum House was that of all the schools Jasper had been to, this was his favourite. At least, it *had* been until now.

'Sorry,' Jasper tried.

'So am I,' the prefect scoffed. 'Sorry I wasn't here to see it.' Then the prefect grabbed Jasper's hand and started shaking it up and down. Jasper felt as though his arm was about to be wrenched from his body.

'All those years of putting up with Bruno and no-one has ever tried anything like that. Awesome. You've got guts. I just wish I'd seen it. Boris, by the way.'

Jasper's brain was still trying to catch up with what he was hearing. 'Um, I'm Jasper. Hi,' he managed.

'Bruno is absolutely spewing. He wouldn't stop going on about it. All holidays he was trying to work out how to get back at you. When I was accepted for my year here, he was stoked. He gave me your picture so I could work out who you were straight away. You should've heard all the things he wanted me to do to you.'

Jasper gulped.

There were actually two schools called the Monstrum House School for Troubled Children. They both looked the same, but were very different. The Monstrum House everyone knew about was a military school. That's where parents thought their 'troubled' kids were sent to be straightened out.

But what most people didn't know was that some of the students were selected to go to another, secret Monstrum House. A Monstrum House where they were taught how to hunt monsters. The two schools didn't usually have anything to do with each other – except for the fact that the biggest, toughest kids from the military school were sent to the monster-hunting school in their last year to be prefects. That's why Bruno was at Jasper's school last year, and why his brother Boris was here now.

'So tell me everything,' said Boris. 'Every detail. I want to –'

'NOW!' yelled Saffy, as she and Felix came bursting through the door. Jasper managed to catch a glimpse of Saffy's furious face before she launched her kickboxing attack into Boris's stomach. Saffy had a lethal kick. So did Felix.

'No, it's OK!' Jasper shouted, but Felix had already swung his foot up to karate kick Boris in the head.

'Yikes,' Felix yelped, hopping backwards as he rubbed his foot.

Revenge!

The last person Felix and Saffy attacked had been knocked out cold, but their kicks bounced off Boris like rubber.

Boris rubbed his head, looking confused.

'Are you, um, OK?' Jasper asked Boris nervously.

Boris looked at Jasper. 'Friends of yours?' he asked quietly.

Jasper nodded, as Saffy and Felix both shook their heads furiously.

Boris turned towards Saffy and Felix. 'Nice to meet you. I'm Boris,' he said, holding out his hand.

Saffy blinked. Felix let out a shocked laugh.

'He's Bruno's brother. But he's nothing like Bruno. Right?' Jasper looked to Boris for assurance.

'I can't stand him. Last year, when he was here, was the best year of my life,' Boris grinned.

A couple of third-year students sauntered out of the food hall. 'Are you serious? A Smurmymorph was living in your basement?' one of them exclaimed. They dropped their voices to a whisper when they noticed Boris, and walked quickly away.

Boris followed them with his gaze. 'A Smurmymorph?' he muttered under his breath. His eyes flicked to Jasper. 'What's going on here? This is a school for serious delinquents, right? Where they send the kids who are too bad for military school. *That's* what this place is supposed to be.'

Jasper looked at Felix and Saffy. 'Um, well,' he stuttered.

'Because, to be honest, none of the kids here seem that bad to me,' Boris continued. 'The kids at the military school I went to last year were far worse than anyone I've seen here so far.'

'Give us time,' Saffy shrugged. She looked sharply at Jasper, who took his cue.

'Yeah, first day back and all,' he added.

'And what is it with this place?' asked Boris. 'It's freezing! And it's so dark, and ... is it just my two-way radio, or is there, like, some creepy whispering going on around the place?'

Jasper froze. Could Boris actually hear the whispering too?

Felix laughed, 'Yeah, Jasper used to go on about some weird whispering, hey, Jasp?'

Jasper mumbled something into his hoodie. He'd learnt last year that the strange whispering he heard was the result of a monster bite. A bite that had infected him with monsterness. And unless he controlled the whispering, he would slowly turn into a monster himself. He hadn't told Saffy and Felix about that yet. Whispering was the first monster characteristic to develop.

Jasper knew there were other kids at school who'd been bitten too – they were called the Whispered. But Boris? A *prefect*?

Saffy shared a look with Felix. 'Maybe it's just your mind playing tricks. Fear will do that to you. This is a pretty cold and spooky place – until you get used to it,' she added.

'I don't scare easily,' Boris said. 'But it is *really* cold.' He was interrupted by his radio crackling to life. He listened intently, and then said, 'Roger that. I'm on my way, sir. Over and out.'

Boris nodded at Jasper, Saffy and Felix. 'Well, duty calls. But McPhee, you owe me a story,' he said, turning and marching away.

As soon as Boris had turned the corner, Saffy took off her shoe and inspected her foot. A massive bruise was blossoming across it. 'Ow! It felt like I kicked a bloomin' brick wall!' she complained.

16

'Last time we come to save you, Jasper,' said Felix. 'You weren't even in trouble.'

'Gee, don't sound so disappointed,' Jasper replied. 'Anyway we have Rest and Relaxation class now, you can both let your pain simply float away. Come on.'

The three of them started down the hallway.

'Who would have thought, hey?' Felix said as they walked towards class. 'Bruno has a brother who isn't a complete bully! Mad.'

'Yeah, but I don't know if we can trust him,' said Saffy. 'It's a bit weird – him asking all those questions about the school.'

'Maybe we should let him know what's going on,' said Jasper, thinking of what Boris had said about the whispering. 'He was pretty nice. And he suspects something. I bet he'll find out sooner or later.'

'Shall I go through *all* the flaws in your

thinking?' Saffy scoffed. 'One, he is a prefect. They don't know about monsters. Which brings me to *two*, they aren't supposed to know about monsters. Three, he would think you were insane, because, honestly, who still believes in monsters at our age? Four, he is too old to see monsters anyway, and five –'

'Unless,' Jasper interrupted, then stopped. *Unless he's been bitten by one*, Jasper thought. *And he is one of the Whispered. Then he'd still be able to see monsters.*

'Unless?' Saffy prodded.

Jasper grinned. 'Unless you're a complete know-it-all who has to be right all the time, pain in the –'

'ATTENTION!' Stenka's voice crackled over the intercom.

The three of them stopped in their tracks. The Monstrum House intercom didn't sound

18

like the normal, tinny sort you heard in most schools. It sounded as though a voice was drilling into your brain.

'All students proceed to the assembly hall immediately for an emergency school assembly. THAT MEANS NOW!'

Felix jumped. 'We'd better go,' he said, and started in the direction of the hall.

'Maybe we'll get out of Rest and Relaxation,' Saffy said to Jasper with a wink.

Jasper hated Rest and Relaxation – the class where their teacher tried to make them relax at the same time as scaring them half out of their wits. But an emergency school meeting?

That really didn't sound good.

The hall was buzzing with anticipation. No-one knew what the assembly was about.

'Emergency assembly? What do you reckon?' Saffy asked.

'I reckon there must be some sort of emergency,' Jasper grinned.

Saffy rolled her eyes.

There was a chuckle from behind them. 'So, they let you back in?'

Jasper's hood was pulled over his eyes by a fourth-year boy in a black hoodie.

'Mac!' Felix cheered.

'Let *us* back in?' Jasper replied, as he squirmed out from under Mac's grip. 'You're the old one. Isn't there an age limit at Monstrum? Are there any other fourth years, or are you the only one immature enough to be allowed back in?'

Mac smiled. 'Ha ha. Actually, there are nine others in my class. But this is it for me. One more year before I can start work in the outside world. I was thinking of joining a tracking crew, but then you have to work night shifts, and I don't know if that's me.'

Felix nudged Jasper. 'That's like your mum, right?'

Jasper nodded. He'd only just found out at the end of last year that his mum wasn't actually a garbage collector, but worked for Monstrum House with their Tracking Department. Instead of spending her mornings driving a truck to pick up rubbish, she was following monsters as they crept through the dark streets. Jasper had been happier thinking she was a garbo.

'So what's all this about then?' Saffy asked Mac.

Mac smiled. 'Have you seen that plant – the one that looks like ivy – that's growing, like, all over the school? I reckon that a Day of Laying might be coming.' Mac clapped his hands in excitement.

'Uh-oh,' Felix groaned. 'He clapped. He's excited. This can't be good.'

Jasper was thinking the same thing. The only time Mac got excited was when he was hunting monsters.

'Ladies and gentlemen!' said a gravelly voice.

Jasper was amazed that he hadn't heard Principal Von Strasser enter the hall. Von

Strasser always rode a horse, even indoors, and usually the clip-clopping was enough to silence everyone. Jasper turned to see the principal wearing a purple samurai outfit and a helmet on his head. He was sitting majestically on top of his horse. And the horse was wearing slippers.

'Nice helmet,' Saffy whispered sarcastically.

'Why thank you, Ms Dominguez.' Von Strasser beamed over the crowd at Saffy, who turned a deep red.

'Welcome, welcome, welcome. Welcome one and all to another exciting year at Monstrum House,' announced the principal. 'As you can see, the first years have not arrived yet, and will not do so for another week. I am sure they're still putting graffiti on walls, stealing cars and other such leisurely activities. But we, *we* have serious work to get down to. Preferably before they arrive.'

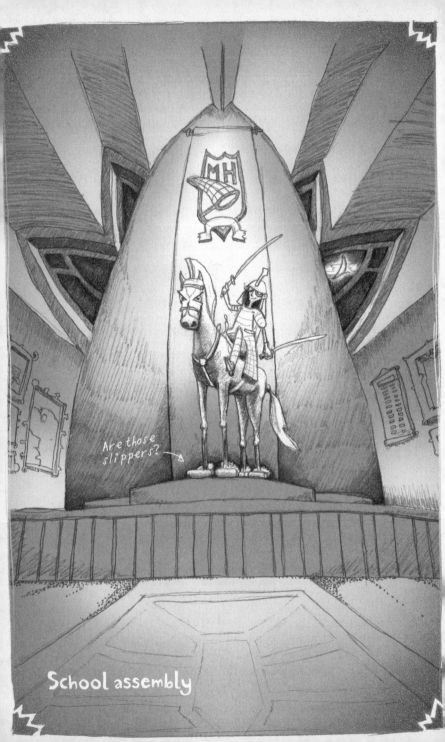

Are those slippers?

School assembly

There were murmurs around the hall.

'SILENCE!' screeched Stenka, the scariest teacher in the school. No-one made a sound.

'I am sorry to say that, once again, the Day of Laying has come upon us,' said Von Strasser.

Mac elbowed Jasper in the ribs.

'In the coming days, a swarm of monsters known as Skrinkerscreech will attempt to infiltrate the school grounds,' continued the principal. 'The Skrinkerscreech are flying, insect-like monsters.' Von Strasser paused. 'Well, I say insect-like, but they are actually about the size of a goat. Or a very small horse. But they look like insects. Quite terrifying, really. In fact, of all the monsters within the Screecher order, I would say that these probably scare me the most. Perhaps it's their oversized stingers, or their fanged mandibles, or the fact that they were the first species of monster to be classed in the Screecher order. Hmmm …' Von Strasser stopped speaking, apparently lost in thought.

Stenka cleared her throat. Their principal looked around in surprise.

'Oh, yes. Here you all are. Of course. Well, then. Keep an eye open for a swarm of flying goat-sized insect-monsters. That's all. Bye for now.' Von Strasser turned his horse around as he waved.

'Wait!' Saffy called out. 'Why are they trying to get into the school?'

Stenka fixed her with a stare.

Von Strasser turned back to face them. 'Thank you, Ms Dominguez. I'm not sure if you've noticed the rather beautiful plant that has recently become rather overgrown around the school? It's screechwort. The Skrinkerscreech nest in it once every five years. They have done so for millennia.'

'Screechwhat?' Jasper whispered to Mac.

'No, *screechwort*,' said Von Strasser. 'It is the Skrinkerscreech's birth plant. All monsters need to feed on their birth plant when they first hatch. Without it, they don't develop any monster characteristics and they can't become monsters. For example, a Grubbergrind would simply be a spider, an Octoglug would be an octopus, et cetera, et cetera. It is something in the birth plant that causes the monster hatchling to mutate and become a monster. The Skrinkerscreech's birth plant is screechwort. And it just so happens that we have a lot of it growing here at Monstrum House.'

Saffy's jaw had dropped open. 'Hang on, so what you're saying is, *inside* the school grounds there's a plant that turns monster hatchlings into monsters?'

Stenka turned to Saffy, looking as if death

rays would shoot from her eyeballs.

'Quite,' Von Strasser nodded.

'And you haven't thought to pull the plant out?' Saffy asked.

'Ms Dominguez!' Stenka exploded.

'Thank you, Stenka,' said Principal Von Strasser. 'But I will explain. Screechwort can't be killed, Ms Dominguez. It's a plant with monster characteristics. It thrives in the cold, dark conditions here. It loves negative feelings. Pulling it out makes it come back twice as big. Spraying it with weed killer makes it grow. Besides, it's quite useful. The leaves are a vital component of many anti-venoms when properly prepared.'

Von Strasser smiled pleasantly. 'There will be nineteen monsters altogether. The queen is particularly impressive. You will need to find her nest and stop her eggs from hatching.

Enjoy your day.' He waved, and trotted out of the hall.

Mac thumped Jasper on the back. 'Cool, huh?' he grinned.

'Yeah,' Jasper replied, 'great.'

Monstrum House wasn't your everyday, run-of-the-mill school. All of the subjects had just one objective: to teach the students how to hunt monsters. Some of the subjects were cool, but Rest and Relaxation wasn't one of them. It was somewhere between a meditation class and an army boot camp.

'Good morning, Class 2B,' the Rest and Relaxation teacher boomed.

'Good morning, Master Poon, sir!' the class replied, as if they were soldiers. Saffy mumbled something else under her breath.

Their teacher, a deranged army general called Master Poon, was sitting cross-legged in the middle of a circle of rose-scented candles. He was dressed in full camouflage gear, complete with a bush on his helmet.

'Now sit,' Master Poon ordered.

The students quickly sat down.

'I have some candles here today to help you all to relax,' yelled Master Poon. 'I want all of you to be very calm. I don't want you to think about your hair catching alight or how horribly your little faces could be disfigured by hot wax. Smell the candles!' he shouted. 'Are you smelling them?'

'Yes, sir!' the class chorused. Saffy rolled her eyes.

'Dominguez! On the floor, give me twenty! No eye-rolling!'

Master Poon

Would YOU feel relaxed if he was your teacher?

He polishes his shoelaces

Saffy gritted her teeth as she finished the twenty push-ups in front of a smirking Felix.

'And Brown! No smirking. Twenty from you!' Master Poon commanded.

Jasper found it really hard not to laugh. He and his friends always had bets about who would have to do the most push-ups in Master Poon's class.

'As well as teaching this class, I will be your homeroom teacher for the year,' Master Poon boomed, once Felix had finished his push-ups. 'So we will be seeing quite a lot of each other. And I will *not* take any nonsense. Now everyone, give me twenty push-ups. That's twenty more for you, Dominguez and Brown. ON THE DOUBLE!'

The whole class started their push-ups while Master Poon surveyed them. 'We are going to have a *great* year. Aren't we, McPhee?'

Jasper looked up to see his teacher staring down at him. Master Poon's eyes flashed spookily in the flickering candlelight.

'Er, yeah, it'll be excellent,' Jasper agreed.

'Now give me another twenty for lying through your teeth,' said Master Poon, pushing Jasper back down onto the floor with his shiny black boot.

Jasper's arms were aching when he sat back on his mat. There couldn't possibly be a worse teacher than Master Poon for a subject called Rest and Relaxation. And the fact that he was their homeroom teacher meant that Jasper would have to see him every day for a whole year. But they had survived Stenka for a year, and Master Poon couldn't be worse than her. *Could he?*

'OK,' said Master Poon. 'Let's relax! Smell those candles! Screechers can feed on your fear

34

and grow stronger. In this class you will learn to keep your cool in the most stressful situations. You will *control* your fear. Are you ready to relax?'

'Yes, sir,' the class mumbled half-heartedly.

'I SAID, ARE YOU READY TO RELAX?'

'Yes, sir!' they shouted.

'I can tell that none of you are relaxing!' said Master Poon. 'Close your eyes and RELAX! Feel your muscles becoming soft. And breathe! Breathe, you maggots!'

Jasper was trying his best to relax, but he knew that any moment, Master Poon would do something worse than just yell at him.

Breathe, said Jasper to himself. *Relax*.

Then Jasper felt something fall softly into his lap. He didn't want to open his eyes. He could already feel the fear creeping in. He'd gone to enough Rest and Relaxation classes to know that whatever was in his lap couldn't be good.

'Keep relaxed, keep calm, control your fear,' said Master Poon sternly. 'And as an added incentive, anyone who *doesn't* scream when they open their eyes gets a cancel card. You can use it to cancel out two penalty points from your record.'

Jasper felt his spirits lift. He could really do with one of those. *How bad can it be?* he thought, almost willing to open his eyes.

But then, the thing in his lap moved. In fact, it *scuttled*.

'Right! Open your eyes,' Master Poon said. 'Now!'

Jasper clenched his teeth together, opened his eyes, and screamed.

The hugest, hairiest, most hideous tarantula Jasper had ever seen was perched on top of his knee.

Everyone in the class was screaming.

'RELAX, you bunch of pansies!' yelled Master Poon.

Every student had something they found horrific in their laps. Jasper leapt to his feet. The spider fell from his knee and scurried under a cupboard.

Master Poon smiled triumphantly and put

the cancel cards back into his pocket as the gong rang for the end of class.

Jasper looked over and saw Felix screaming at a brussels sprout. He shook his head. He grabbed Felix and wrenched him to his feet. They didn't speak as they ran out into the hallway. None of the other kids in the class followed.

'He hadn't dismissed us,' groaned Felix.

'I don't care. My skin was crawling. I had to get out of there,' said Jasper.

Saffy arrived a few minutes later. 'Barbie doll,' she shuddered. 'I didn't like dolls much when I was little.'

Jasper couldn't help laughing. 'You're as bad as Felix. No card then?' he asked. Saffy didn't respond.

A bunch of prefects came clomping down the hallway towards them.

'Hey, losers,' one of them snarled. 'All you

pieces of dog drool had better get to class before you make me make you ... make ... yeah.'

'How do you get a *piece* of drool?' Saffy asked.

The prefect looked confused for a moment, then handed Saffy a penalty card. 'Make that two penalty points, drool-head.'

Saffy flashed him a pretty smile. 'Afraid not,' she replied and reached into the pocket of her hoodie. 'Suck on this.' She shoved a cancel card into the prefect's hand and turned on her heel.

Jasper and Felix charged after Saffy. They knew from past experience that the prefects weren't choosy about who they punished. Jasper pitied the poor student who ran into that prefect next.

'You got a card? How did you get a card?' Felix asked as they caught up to Saffy.

Saffy ignored Felix and kept on walking.

'Hurry up. I don't want to be late. We've got private tutorials now.'

Jasper looked questioningly at Felix. 'Huh?'

Saffy stopped at a large noticeboard. It was covered in papers, pinned on with some weird-looking drawing pins. Jasper leant in closely and saw the pinheads looked a lot like tiny human heads.

'If you two hadn't run off so quickly, you would've heard Master Psycho back there explain,' Saffy replied. She pointed to the board. 'He had two announcements. The first is that we have a test next class.'

Felix and Jasper both groaned.

'Not the Trail of Terror, please not the Trail of Terror,' Felix begged.

Saffy nodded. 'Yep. He's already set it up with our fears.'

The Trail of Terror was the test all the students

dreaded. Jasper, Saffy and Felix hadn't done one yet, but the older kids had warned them about it. It took place in a room that was a bit like a maze. The path through the room was narrow and full of twists and turns. And around every corner waited the worst fear of each student in the class. The students had to make it through the room to the door at the other end. As a test of teamwork, every single student in the class had to make it through. If just one kid failed, the whole class had to do it again. Jasper just hoped that the rest of his class were frightened of brussels sprouts, like Felix. *That* he could handle.

'Saffy,' said Felix, 'you still haven't told us how you got that cancel card.'

Saffy ignored Felix again and turned to the noticeboard. 'The second announcement was that now we're in second year, we've all been put in individual tutorials depending on our strengths,' she said. 'They're twice a week, after our Rest and Relaxation class.' Saffy pointed to the noticeboard. 'Better find out where we're supposed to be.'

Jasper searched the notices for his name. He found it, held with a drawing pin that looked as though it was crying out in pain. Jasper hoped that didn't say anything about how painful his tutorial would be. Next to his name, he read: Memory Modification – Room 13.

Jasper frowned. *Memory Modification*. He thought he'd heard Von Strasser mention it before, but he had no idea what it was. He felt a bit let down – he'd been hoping for Mental Manipulation with Mr Golag. That was his best subject. He wondered if he could switch.

'Cool! Functional Fixedness!' exclaimed Saffy. 'Just wait, I'm going to invent the coolest gadgets ever. James Bond, eat your heart out. Once the secret service sees what I come up with, they'll be *begging* me to work for them.'

Jasper could see the plans already forming in Saffy's head. If anyone could invent a cool spy gadget using only old bits of rubbish, it was Saffy.

Felix found his name and groaned. 'Please let this be a mistake,' he said.

'What is it?' Saffy asked.

'Species Studies.' Felix shook his head in despair.

Jasper laughed. 'Lucky you!' he teased. 'You get extra one-on-one classes twice a week with Stenka!'

Felix looked pained. 'But we've *all* got Species Studies later. I'll have double Stenka! Why me?'

'Because it's what you're good at,' said Saffy.

'Hey, without you, we never would've passed the Task last year,' she reminded him. 'What about you, what are you supposedly good at, Jasp?'

Jasper shrugged his shoulders as Saffy found his name on the board.

'What's Memory Modification?' she asked. 'Is that like some sort of Mental Manipulation stream? Sounds cool.'

Jasper shrugged again. He'd started private classes with Señor Hermes last year to help control his monster side. All the Whispered kids at the school did them. The classes were secret, so Jasper wondered if Memory Modification was just a code name. Maybe he just had a class with Señor Hermes.

'Don't know,' said Jasper. 'But whatever it is – I guess I'm about to find out.'

Jasper knocked on the door to Room 13.

'No knocking, dude,' a strange voice called from inside. 'It kills my karma, man.'

Jasper paused. This was weird. He was sure he knew all the teachers at Monstrum House. Even the ones who hadn't taught him yet. But this voice was definitely not familiar.

Jasper nudged the door open with his foot. He still wasn't convinced that Memory Modification was a real class. Maybe Señor Hermes was playing some evil kind of trick to keep him on his toes.

Jasper peered inside the room, and felt his jaw drop open. A guy in sunglasses, a tie-dyed T-shirt and loose cotton trousers was lounging on a beach chair in the middle of the room.

Nope, definitely not Hermes. The guy's hair was waist-length and tied in a plait. He took off his sunnies and smiled as Jasper entered.

'Hey, like, welcome, little dude,' the guy said. He sipped at some kind of tropical drink in a tall glass with a flower poking out the top.

'Um, h-hi,' Jasper stammered.

'Call me Mr Ż.' The guy waved and patted the empty beach chair next to him.

'What's the Z stand for?' Jasper asked.

'Just Mr Z is cool, dig?'

Jasper wasn't entirely sure what the guy had just said, but he nodded. 'Yeah, right.'

'Anyway, just ease back, let hang, loosen up

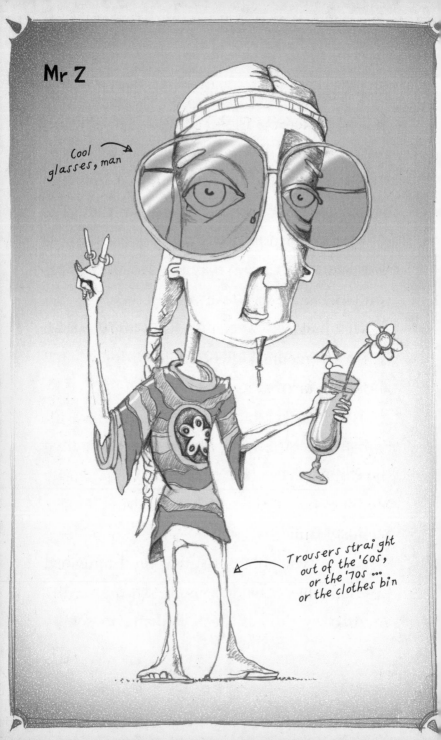

your mind, man.' Mr Z put his sunglasses back on and picked up a guitar. 'We're going to try and find your tune,' he said.

'My *what*?' This guy seemed way too chilled out to be a teacher at Monstrum House. Jasper wondered if it was some sort of trap. 'What is Memory Modification anyway? And who *are* you? I've never seen you before.'

Mr Z looked at Jasper over his sunnies. 'Not that you remember,' he said.

Jasper stared at him.

'The Golagster told me you were well set with your Mental Manipulations stuff. So I said we should see if you could handle some Memory Modification. This class is, like, super-duper Mental Manip. Plus, 'cos you were done by a Scrambler, you should be right on the money, 'cos Scramblers get into people's heads, yeah? You in?'

So Saffy was right. Cool. Jasper found himself grinning. 'All right!'

'Right on, man.' Mr Z nodded his approval. He plucked a few notes on his guitar. 'Try whistling me a tune.'

Jasper tried to think of a tune but his mind was blank. 'I can't think of anything,' said Jasper.

Mr Z peered at Jasper over the top of his sunglasses. He played a little ditty on his guitar.

While Mr Z played, the theme from *Sesame Street* popped into Jasper's head. He shrugged and started whistling.

Mr Z lay back in his beach chair and grinned. 'That's it, man!' he cheered. 'That's your tune!'

'What's that mean?' asked Jasper. 'How does it work?' He was a bit worried that 'his tune' was from a little kids' TV show. *Why couldn't*

I have thought of something cool, like ... like ...

But even now, nothing was coming to him except *Sesame Street*.

'Dude,' said Mr Z. 'It's like, you can use Memory Modification to help people forget the bad vibes. If you get your tune right, you can, like, cover over the bad with the good. So fears just vanish away. They float off into the sunset. It's deep.'

That sounded awesome. But Jasper had another question. 'Why are you so different from all the other teachers here?' he asked. 'I mean, have you been bitten, like the rest of them? 'Cos you don't seem to have much of a monster side.'

Mr Z laughed. 'Hey, dude. I was done by a Scrambler like you. I've got a monster side, but it's all about making peace with it, yeah? My monster side loves getting into people's heads, and I can use that in my job. I'm in control of the whispering. I can twist it around so that instead of driving people crazy, I'm like, helping them forget their fears. It doesn't have to be a bad thing, yeah?'

Jasper was starting to agree. He licked his lips and started whistling again, with Mr Z joining in on the guitar. Jasper hadn't felt this good in ages. They worked on Jasper's tune until the gong went for the end of class, interrupting them mid-chorus.

'Oh, man,' Mr Z shook his head sadly. 'That gong is such a downer.'

'But – I feel like I only just got here!' said Jasper.

'As far as you can remember,' said Mr Z with a wink. 'Good going, Jasperlator. Till next time. Yo.'

Jasper stepped out of Room 13 on a high. But as soon as he checked his timetable, his heart sank. Species Studies with Stenka. He didn't want to be late. He ran towards the Species Studies classroom, turned a corner and crashed head-first into someone rushing from the other direction. He was knocked to the ground. The ceiling swirled, then everything went black.

'Jasper? Can you hear me? Are you OK?' The voice sounded as though it were coming from a long way away.

Jasper's head pounded. He groaned and opened his eyes. Boris was peering anxiously down at him.

'Yeah, couldn't be better,' Jasper managed to gasp. He felt as though he'd just walked into a bus.

Boris helped Jasper to his feet.

'Why were you in such a hurry?' Jasper asked, gingerly feeling the bump on his head with his fingertips.

Boris shook his head furiously and clamped his lips shut.

Jasper looked at Boris. He knew that look. Total fear and disbelief. The look that every first-year had on their face when Principal Von Strasser showed them the Blibberwail on their first day, as proof that monsters existed. 'You've seen one, haven't you?' asked Jasper.

Boris's eyes narrowed. 'Seen one *what*?'

'You know what. A monster.' Jasper hoped he was right about Boris or else he'd sound like a complete loony.

Boris turned pale. 'No, I didn't. Because I couldn't have. Because monsters aren't real. Because if they *were* real, and if they were here, then Bruno would've told me, and, and there is all this whispering all the time, and … What is this stupid place anyway?!' he exploded.

Jasper nodded. 'Yep, you saw one. Don't worry, the panic eases off soon. The best thing to do is just accept it.'

Boris's eyes were darting all over the place. 'But it was so horrible. It had this long tongue and three noses. And why was the Principal taking it for a walk *on a leash*?'

Definitely the Blibberwail, Jasper decided. 'It's a trained monster. It lives in the basement, but every now and then Von Strasser takes it out for a walk. That's one of the ways he makes it less monsterish, so he can train it. By being nice to it,' Jasper explained.

Boris looked completely confused. It all sounded perfectly normal to Jasper, but then, he *had* been learning about monsters for the last year. There was no way Boris could understand it all in one go.

'OK, first off,' said Jasper, 'monsters *are* real. Everyone knows that as a kid. It's just that when people get older, they stop seeing them. It's all to do with shrinkage – of the brain,' he clarified.

Boris was breathing in short, sharp gasps.

'When you get older, your brain shrinks. And that's why most people can't see them anymore. But *you* can still see them, and you're older.'

Boris was pacing up and down. 'This is just

too weird. There's no way ...'

Jasper wasn't sure what to say next. When Señor Hermes had told him about the whispering last year, he was completely freaked out. And he still didn't really want anyone to know about it. But if Boris was a Whispered too, then he had to know about it, or he'd become a monster himself.

Jasper took a deep breath. 'You said you can hear whispering. So I think you might've been bitten by a monster. When you were a kid or something,' Jasper said slowly.

'I don't know what you're talking about,' said Boris.

'If you *were* bitten by a monster,' Jasper continued slowly, 'then you're like me. A Whispered. It means that you have this stuff called monsterness inside you and –'

Boris clapped his hand over Jasper's mouth.

'Stop,' he said. 'This can't be true.'

Jasper shrugged. Boris slowly took his hand away.

'Look,' Jasper tried again. 'You've been hearing some creepy whispering, right?'

'Yeah, maybe,' said Boris quietly. 'But I don't know what it's saying.'

'That's the first stage. Whispering is the first monster characteristic to develop. You've got to learn to control the whispering. If you don't, you will turn more and more, well, monsterish.' Jasper tried to look reassuring, and not to think about what might happen in the next stages.

'Monsterish?' asked Boris, his face turning even paler.

'Yes,' said Jasper. 'You're kind of … becoming a monster. The whispering you can hear is your monster side trying to guide you. But you can control it.'

Becoming a monster

Stage 1

Stage 2

Stage 3

'Contol. Right. Good,' said Boris, trying to gather himself together. 'I'm good at control. So, what do I do? Push-ups? Sit-ups? Marching? I'll walk all night if I have to.'

'You'll have to talk to Señor Hermes. I'll take you there. And maybe we should tell Stenka too,' Jasper conceded.

Boris shook his head. 'No way. *You can't tell anyone!*' he said forcefully. 'I can't go to one of your teachers. I'm pretty sure I'm not supposed to know about the whole monster thing. None of the other prefects do. The teachers will kick me out for knowing about it. It'll be the end of the line for me. My family would never understand. They would kill me. They'd never talk to me again. I would be homeless. I would –'

Jasper held up his hand to stop Boris mid-panic. 'OK, I get it. But I'm sure they won't kick you out.' Yet, even as Jasper said it, he had to wonder. The whole reason the prefects were there was because they *couldn't* see monsters. They couldn't be scared or affected by them. Maybe Boris could become a student? Although he *was* pretty old. His brain must have started shrinking already. Jasper didn't meet Boris's gaze.

'Can't you help me? You can hear the whispering too, right?' Boris was looking desperate.

Jasper wanted to help, but he was only just learning how to control his own whisper. He didn't know if he could help someone else. 'You know, I'm really not that good at it. You would be much better off –'

Boris punched the wall in frustration, leaving a large fist-sized hole next to Jasper's head.

'Sorry!' Boris gasped. 'I've never done that

before! I just feel so, so frustrated and angry! See? That must be my monster side! It's coming! It's getting worse! Aaaaargh!' Boris punched another hole in the wall. 'Yikes!' he yelped. 'I did it again. I'm really, really sorry! You've gotta help me. I can count on you, can't I?' Boris pleaded.

'OK! OK!' said Jasper, looking at the two holes in the wall. It didn't look like he had much choice.

'Dog drool,' Stenka pointed to the large flasks of murky liquid stacked along the wall.

Jasper collapsed into the comfy couch next to the fire. Felix put down the flask in his hand.

'Gross!' Felix whispered, wiping his hand on his hoodie.

'At this moment, the prefects are tempting every single dog on campus with pieces of steak, and carefully collecting their saliva,' Stenka explained. 'I imagine they are looking for someone to assist them, so if I were you,

I would tread very carefully.' She peered around the class of students. No-one moved.

'McPhee!' she barked. Jasper flinched. 'Can you tell me *why* the prefects are collecting dog saliva? And keep in mind, the wrong answer will be rewarded with an hour of drool-collecting.'

Because that's all they're good for, was the first response that entered Jasper's head. But since coming to Monstrum House, Jasper had learnt not to act on impulse. Not all the time anyway. 'Because that is the Skrinkerscreech's weakness?' he suggested.

Stenka looked disappointed. 'Exactly. Dog saliva has the ability to freeze a Skrinkerscreech solid. As of now, you are all required to wear your hunt belts, and to carry a flask of dog drool with you at all times. It is not to be taken off. Not in the shower, not in bed, not anywhere. Anyone found without their drool will be

The hunt belt

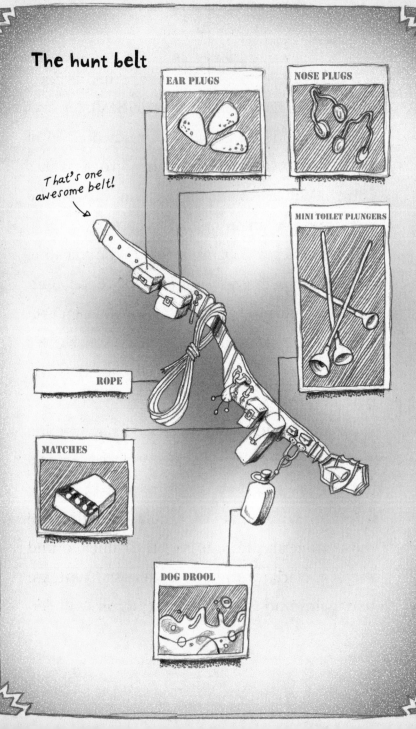

EAR PLUGS

NOSE PLUGS

That's one awesome belt!

MINI TOILET PLUNGERS

ROPE

MATCHES

DOG DROOL

severely dealt with,' she added with menace.

'To catch the monsters before the queen lays her eggs, you will all need to be at the top of your game. As I haven't seen the top of anyone's game in the last year, I hold grave fears for the success of this mission. So listen.'

Jasper's leg was burning next to the crackling fire. He desperately wanted to move his chair away, but he didn't want to draw attention to himself and interrupt Stenka's speech. He decided that catching on fire was probably the better option.

'Skrinkerscreech fly in a swarm surrounding the queen,' Stenka said as she paced up and down the room. 'While you need to catch the queen and her eggs, it is the drones that are most dangerous to you. It is their duty to find the best place for the queen to nest. There are two things that the Skrinkerscreech queen needs to lay her eggs. One,' Stenka cracked her stick against the board, 'she needs a plentiful supply of screechwort from which to make her nest. Two,' she cracked her stick again, 'she needs an environment that is full of fear. If the drones do not find a suitable site, they will *make* a place fearful.'

Stenka eyeballed the students one by one. 'Your aim is to find the nest and get the eggs before the hatchlings can eat the screechwort. Without being attacked, obviously. The queen herself is quite harmless, yet she is mesmerising and powerful. But her eighteen drones will not wait to be provoked before they attack. They will do anything to protect her. Their antennae are able to sense any kind of threat to the queen.'

'Stenka,' said Felix. 'Er, what happens if we get attacked?'

'The sting from a Skrinkerscreech is very

painful, Mr Brown. Within seconds, the victim erupts into hives. The hives fill with pus and burst. The victim then has open wounds leaking fluid from their bodies. It's a hideous sight, made worse by the fact that the hives also contain a paralysing fear gas. When the hives pop, anyone close to the victim will become paralysed with fear. And once you are paralysed, it is not easy to escape the Skrinkerscreech.'

Stenka looked particularly pleased with the response rippling around the room.

There was a sharp rap on the door. Stenka turned. 'ENTER!'

A prefect marched into the room. It was the same prefect Saffy had given her cancel card to earlier in the day. He saluted Stenka and handed her a rolled-up note. As he was leaving, he spotted Felix, Jasper and Saffy by the fire. His eyes narrowed nastily.

'Gee, thanks a lot, Saffy,' Felix whispered as soon as the prefect had left. 'That's just what we need. Now monsters are taking over the school *and* the thug brigade is out to get us. Couldn't you have just taken the penalty points?'

'Mr Brown, unless you have a passion for collecting dog saliva, I suggest you refrain from speaking in my class,' said Stenka, her voice like ice.

Felix's mouth clamped shut and he shrank into his chair.

'I have just received a red alert.' Stenka glanced down at the note in her hand. 'The Skrinkerscreech swarm has been detected inside the Monstrum House grounds. As of now, all classes are cancelled. You will be formed into emergency hunt crews. It is imperative that you catch the queen. Listen for a low buzzing – the sound of the monsters' wings. You will hear it four seconds before being attacked. Although, if you hear buzzing, I imagine it will be too late to do much.'

Stenka crushed the note in her hand. 'Use the dog drool wisely. Unfortunately, until the capture of the monsters, the teachers will have to keep a low profile. We will communicate with the prefects in the case of an emergency. But you students will be on your own, as on any other Hunt.'

'On our own? So, if we catch a monster, what are we supposed to do with it?' Saffy demanded.

'There will be older students on hand to direct the disposal of caught monsters,' Stenka replied. She handed Saffy a penalty card with two points on it. 'And don't question me.' Stenka smiled nastily.

Saffy didn't miss a beat. She pulled a cancel

card from her pocket. 'I'll use this then,' she said, matching Stenka's smile.

Felix and Jasper turned to each other. *Two cards?* How on earth had Saffy managed to get *two* cards?

Stenka scowled. 'Master Poon and his cancel cards,' Stenka muttered. She took the card, eyeing Saffy suspiciously. 'You must have impressed him, Ms Dominguez. I will ask him why he's rewarded you.'

Saffy shrugged.

'Right, you, you, you and you,' Stenka pointed to four students. 'Crew 1.'

She continued to break the students into crews. Felix and Saffy ended up together, but Jasper was stuck in a separate crew.

'Maybe you can swap?' Felix suggested.

'No swapping! Now move!' Stenka yelled.

Jasper shrugged. 'Guess not. Good luck,' he

said to Felix, who looked as though he wanted to throw up.

'You too,' Saffy said. 'Oh, and here.' She shoved a squashed tin can into Jasper's hand. 'My first attempt at Functional Fixedness. It might come in handy now we're not together.' Saffy turned the can over, revealing a small red button. 'Walkie-talkies,' she grinned.

Jasper's eyes grew wide. 'Are you serious?' he asked. But Saffy was already pulling Felix out of the classroom to catch up with their crew. 'Don't forget your dog drool,' she called.

Jasper turned to find Stenka towering over him. He shoved the tin-can invention into his pocket.

'Crew 4, over here,' Stenka ordered. The other members of the crew looked as worried as Jasper felt.

'You won't be hunting,' Stenka said quietly.

'Find Señor Hermes, in Room 10. He will explain. I need to round up the other Whispered students.' She turned and strode away.

Jasper and the other three stood uncertainly in the now-empty room. 'You guys are all Whispered too?' he asked.

They all looked at each other, and nodded.

'Well, that explains that,' Jasper said. 'But why on earth aren't we allowed to hunt?'

Señor Hermes was waiting outside Room 10.

'Quickly!' he ordered, ushering Jasper and the others into the room.

The room was already half-full of students from other classes and year levels. Four or five of the school's dogs were mingling among the students. Jasper recognised Woof from last year. Woof wagged his tail and bounded over to Jasper. He was an awesome dog. Somehow, he always seemed to understand what Jasper was saying.

Woof!

He loves a good leg to chew on

A monster-hunter's best friend

'Hey, fella,' Jasper whispered into Woof's ear. 'What's going on, hey?' Woof licked him in response.

Mac pushed his way through the students towards Jasper. He looked worried.

'Something's wrong,' Mac said quietly. 'I wasn't around for the last Day of Laying, but I don't get why we've been shoved in here. We're the ones who know how to find the monsters. We need to be out *there*!'

Jasper had never seen Mac look so agitated.

Señor Hermes hurried the last few students through the door before slamming it shut and bolting it.

'All right, settle down,' Señor Hermes said softly. Jasper noticed that even Hermes seemed on edge. Jasper was beginning to feel nervous himself.

'What's going on? Why are we all stuck in

here?' Mac called out. There were murmurs of agreement from some of the other students.

Hermes held up his hand for silence. 'I know,' he said, 'you want to be out there catching the monsters. But this is one Hunt you all have to sit out.'

Mac shook his head. 'No way! This is when we're needed the most!' he protested.

'When it is nesting, the Skrinkerscreech is a particularly vicious, protective and territorial species,' Hermes explained over the complaints. 'They don't just frighten off potential threats. They *kill* them. Monsters don't usually fight amongst themselves, but at nesting time, some species become more aggressive.'

'But aren't the others in danger?' Jasper asked, trying not to think about Felix and Saffy.

'The others are only in danger of being stung and severely frightened. The Skrinkerscreech's aggressive streak is reserved for other monsters. Their antennae are designed to detect other monsters in their nesting grounds, and, well ...' Señor Hermes gestured to the students gathered in the room. He didn't need to finish the sentence.

We are all part-monster, Jasper realised. *And that's why there are no teachers on the Hunt. They're all at risk too.*

'I take it you have all heard of the Reversal Room,' Hermes added. 'It is where monsters are taken once they're caught to be, essentially, de-monstered. The room is warm and light, and the monsters are pampered to within an inch of their lives. The more love they are given, the less monster they become. That is where we must go.'

A few kids looked perked up by this news. None of the students had ever been in Reversal

Room before.

'It's the one room in the school where we know the Skrinkerscreech and their birth plant can't infiltrate. Screechwort needs the dark, icy, harsh environment of Monstrum House to grow, and the Skrinkerscreech could never nest there as there's too much good feeling,' Hermes explained.

Mac still looked disgruntled. Jasper figured that he wanted to get in as much hunting as he could in his last year.

Jasper scratched Woof behind the ears. 'Did those dumb prefects get much drool from you?' he asked, then froze.

The prefects! Boris!

Jasper had to get word to Boris. He was in serious danger. Jasper looked at the bolted door. He was trapped. Woof licked his hand reassuringly.

'Since when have I ever let a locked door stop me, hey, boy?' Jasper grinned.

He walked quickly to Señor Hermes. 'Um, I really need to pee.' Jasper tried to look embarrassed.

Hermes shook his head. 'You will have to wait. I'm just waiting for word that everyone is in place, and then we leave.'

Jasper crossed his legs. 'But I *really* have to go.'

Hermes looked at him sharply. 'Jasper, I'm warning you. I don't want you doing anything stupid. If the monsters find you, they will kill you.'

Jasper put on his best anxious face. 'It's either in the toilet or on the floor. What if I take one of the dogs with me?' he suggested. Woof wagged his tail.

Hermes looked at his watch. 'If you step one

81

toe out of line, you'll have me to answer to. Matheson!' Hermes turned to a fourth-year student. 'Can you please accompany young McPhee here to the toilet? We wouldn't want any accidents.'

Jasper smiled, but Hermes didn't appear to get the joke. Jasper didn't know Matheson very well, but he didn't look friendly.

Hermes turned to Woof. 'Guard!' he said, pointing at Jasper.

Woof seemed to grow in size. He turned to Jasper and snarled, as if to show Hermes that he wouldn't take any nonsense. Hermes quickly unbolted the door, and checked the hallway before shooing Jasper, Matheson and Woof out.

The door slammed shut behind them. Woof growled again. Jasper heard the bolt slide shut. He was beginning to wonder if this was such a good idea.

Matheson pulled Jasper down the hallway. 'Hurry up,' he said impatiently. 'I don't want to die for your weak bladder.' Matheson stopped at the door to the toilets. 'The dog can go in with you to guard. I'll keep watch out here. If you hear anything, don't come out. Just run. There's a door on the other side of the bathroom. It's the only other exit.'

Jasper gulped. This was getting scary.

Woof followed Jasper into the toilets. He seemed to know what Jasper was thinking. He stopped growling and yipped excitedly. Jasper gave him a pat. 'Wait until I'm out of sight, then sound the alarm. I don't want Matheson in danger.'

Jasper tipped his head back and stared at the vent in the roof. He had been in this bathroom before and he knew of a way out that Matheson didn't. In his first year he'd discovered a tunnel leading from outside the building right to the vent above him. He just had to climb up into the tunnel, then follow it until he reached the exit. It would take less than ten minutes.

Jasper climbed up onto the sink, working the vent free with his fingers. The vent made a horrible grating noise, which Jasper tried to cover by coughing.

'Hurry up!' Matheson called.

'Coming!' Jasper replied. He grabbed onto the vent with both hands. The metal dug painfully into his palms. He jumped as high as he could, hauling himself through the vent and into the roof. Woof wagged his tail approvingly.

Jasper carefully closed the vent. He peered into the dark tunnel. Woof sounded the alarm. Jasper saw him barking madly at the door on the opposite side of the bathroom. 'Clever dog,' Jasper whispered.

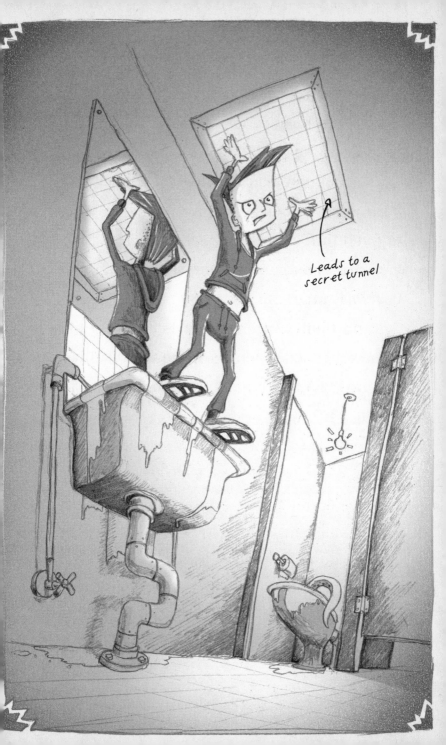

Leads to a secret tunnel

He started silently down the tunnel. He knew he'd be in serious trouble, but he *had* to find Boris.

Jasper knew exactly where the tunnel would take him. It ended not far from the forest, around the back of the school.

There was a little door at the end of the tunnel that led outside.

And then Jasper remembered that the last time he'd used this tunnel, the door had been covered in a plant that looked suspiciously like ivy.

Jasper opened the small door and scraped away the screechwort surrounding the door. He tried to tap into his whispering to find out if the swarm of killer monsters was near by. But he couldn't hear anything, not even a low buzzing sound. Jasper decided this was a good sign and crawled out of the tunnel. An ice-cold wind whipped around him.

Find Boris and get back. That was as far as Jasper's plan had got. But now he realised that Boris could be anywhere. On guard duty near the fence, in the school herding students, collecting dog drool. Jasper might never find him.

A cheer rose up from around the other side of the school. Jasper listened, catching sounds of excitement in the wind. Had the swarm of monsters been caught already?

Jasper edged his way around the side of the building. The wind picked up the snow, making it impossible to see. Something crackled unpleasantly in his pocket.

'Crcckasper! Crccckom in! Crrkover,' Saffy's tinny voice echoed from Jasper's hoodie. *The walkie-talkie!* Jasper realised. It actually worked. Jasper pulled the squashed tin can from his pocket.

'Ow!' he yelped as an electric shock shot up his arm. Saffy obviously hadn't perfected Functional Fixedness yet. 'Saffy? Come in.

Walkie-talkies

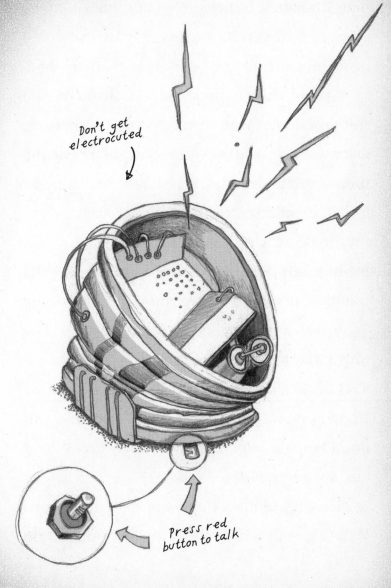

Don't get
electrocuted

Press red
button to talk

Saffy? Over.' Jasper held the walkie-talkie gingerly between his fingers.

'Where arckre you? Crrkover,' Saffy replied.

'At the edge of the forest. I'm in the rim of trees opposite Light Tower 3. I'm on my own. Over.' Jasper had no idea how much of the message Saffy could hear. He waited anxiously for a few minutes.

Then a rock hit Jasper painfully in the back of the neck. He turned to see Saffy and Felix grinning at him. 'I knew you had to be close,' Saffy waved the walkie-talkie at Jasper. 'They only have a range of thirty metres.'

'I can't believe you actually made a –' Jasper stopped short. He was staring at Felix, who was munching slowly on a bar of chocolate. 'Where did you get that?'

'They brought us some chocolate to keep us feeling good,' said Felix. 'Just like on a Hunt.

They had wheelbarrows full of the stuff in the courtyard.'

That explained the cheering Jasper had heard.

Felix grinned, his teeth coated in chocolate. 'Pockets are full.' He shook his hoodie.

'Can I have some?' Japser pleaded. Felix threw him a bar.

'What's going on?' Saffy asked Jasper. 'Señor Hermes sent the thug brigade after you. *All* of them are looking for you. Even Boris came asking. He said to tell you to turn yourself in.'

'If the other prefects get hold of you, you'll wish you were caught by the monsters,' said Felix.

'We knew we had to find you,' Saffy explained. 'So we said we'd go out and gather screechwort for the big nest.'

'The what?' asked Jasper.

'The big nest,' Saffy repeated. 'It was my idea – to, you know, entice the monsters into the assembly hall. I figured that if we got a huge pile of screechwort and put it all together in one place with heaps of fearful vibes, what monster could resist? This way, we bring the monsters to us, rather than us going to them. And then we trap them,' she finished. 'Where have you been? And what have you done?'

Jasper had a lot of explaining to do. But he shook his head. 'We have to find Boris. He's in danger. I'll tell you on the way.'

Saffy nodded towards the fence line of Monstrum House. 'Boris said he would check out the perimeter,' she said, leading the way. 'Now start explaining.'

Jasper took a deep breath. 'OK, well, you know last year, when Von Strasser mentioned that thing about people who'd been bitten by a monster?' Jasper couldn't meet his friends' eyes. He really hoped this wouldn't change things between them. After all, he was about to tell them that he was part-monster.

'Yeah …' Saffy prodded.

'Well,' Jasper paused, 'it's like, um, I mean, ah …'

Felix started laughing. 'We already know, don't worry about it.' He thumped Jasper on the back.

Saffy shook her head. 'You could have dragged it out a bit, Felix,' she huffed.

Jasper stopped walking. 'Hang on, you know, about me being a Whispered?'

Saffy and Felix nodded. 'It was *so* obvious,' Saffy replied. 'We just wanted to see how long it took for you to tell your best buddies. Speaking of which,' Saffy turned to Felix, 'you owe me ten bucks. He told us way sooner than you thought he would.'

Felix mumbled something under his breath.

Jasper felt as though a huge weight had been lifted off his shoulders. 'So, you don't care?'

'Duh,' Saffy said. 'To be honest, I'm kind of jealous. I'm considering getting myself bitten so I can have some super-duper monster-hunting edge as well.'

'It's pretty cool,' agreed Felix. 'But I think I can do without getting bitten.'

They were almost at the fence line. Jasper thought he could make out Boris by the fence, but it was getting dark. The last thing he wanted to do was waltz up to one of the other prefects and get dragged back to Señor Hermes, while Boris was left in danger of being killed by a Skrinkerscreech.

Felix froze. 'Hang on. You shouldn't be out here, Jasper!' he said. 'And Boris? You think he's a Whispered too?'

Jasper nodded.

'What's going on?' asked Saffy.

'Skrinkerscreeches,' Felix said. 'They are particularly vicious and kill other monsters anywhere near their nesting place. Which means the Whispered are all in trouble.'

Jasper looked at Felix in awe. He suddenly realised why Felix was having extra Species Studies classes. He really did have a brain for this sort of stuff.

'You need to get inside.' Felix looked terrified. 'Their antennae are really powerful. They'll sense your monster side in no time.'

Jasper didn't need reminding. 'Which is why we need to warn Boris. Now.'

Felix and Saffy crunched through the snow towards the prefect, while Jasper hung back. Jasper hoped that Saffy had some more of the cancel cards with her. Students weren't supposed to venture this far from the school unsupervised. If the prefect turned out to be anyone other than Boris, Saffy and Felix would get in trouble – but Jasper would be delivered straight back to Señor Hermes.

The coast was clear.

Saffy stuck two fingers in her mouth and

whistled loudly for Jasper. He emerged from the trees, and Boris strode purposefully towards him.

Jasper smiled. 'Thank goodness it's you.'

Boris sighed. 'Sorry, mate,' he said, then threw Jasper into the snow, knocking the wind out of him.

'You are now under prefect arrest. You don't have to say anything, but anything you do say may be given in evidence. You don't have the right to do anything except what you're told. If you do not comply, this may be a painful experience,' Boris recited.

'Boris, listen!' Jasper wheezed. 'I can explain! But you have to let me go!'

Saffy and Felix were standing with their mouths hanging open.

Boris shook his head. 'I'm afraid I can't do that. As much as I would like to help you out,

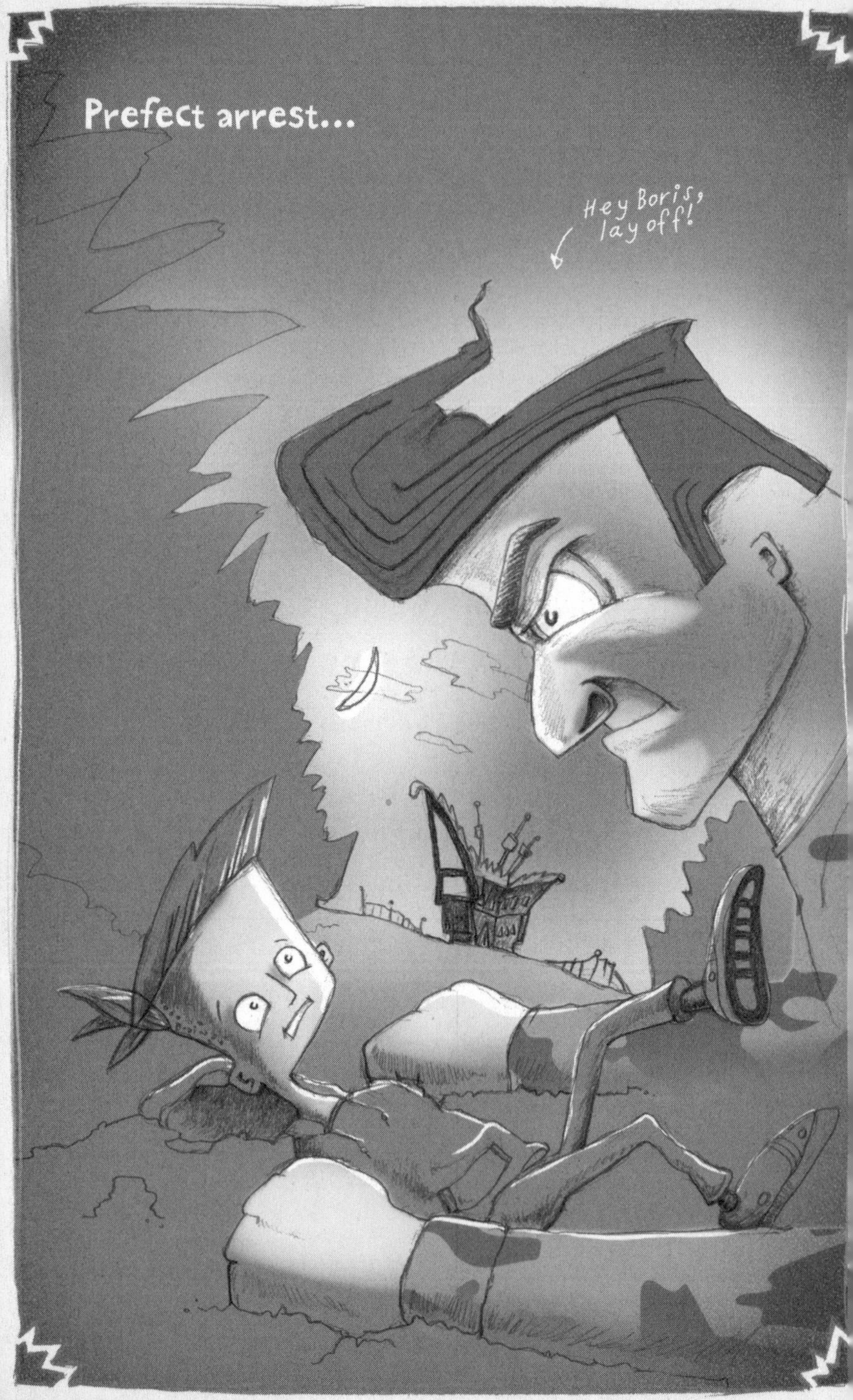
Prefect arrest...
Hey Boris, lay off!

I have my orders. And my orders clearly state to apprehend you and take you back to the mansion using any force necessary.'

Saffy held up her hand. 'OK, OK. You don't have to disobey your orders. But you can still let Jasper go.'

'I'm not stupid,' said Boris.

Saffy didn't seem convinced about that, and Jasper hoped that she wouldn't argue the point. 'I know,' she said instead. 'But your orders said "by any force necessary", right?'

Boris nodded slowly.

'Well, if it isn't necessary to use *any* force, then you could let him go, couldn't you? If he promises to go back to the mansion with you?'

Boris thought about that for a few moments.

'If you try to run, I *will* chase you down,' Boris warned.

Jasper nodded. 'I promise, no running.'

99

Boris let go of Jasper's arm and helped him to his feet.

'Let's go,' Boris commanded, shoving Jasper towards the mansion.

'Gladly,' Jasper said. 'This is why I had to escape from Señor Hermes, so you and I could go back to the mansion together.'

Boris stopped walking. 'That really doesn't make sense.'

Jasper looked to Saffy and Felix. He had no idea how to tell Boris that a swarm of monsters was out to kill him. Well, to kill them both, really, but Jasper was trying not to think about that bit.

Saffy took control. 'Boris,' she said seriously, 'you know about monsters, right?'

Boris looked at Jasper. 'They know?'

Jasper shrugged. 'Of course. They know all about it. They even know you're a Whispered.'

Boris stared intently at Jasper. 'I told you not to –'

'The problem is,' Saffy interrupted, 'there's like this whole bunch of flying monsters. And they're in the school to lay monster eggs. Which is why we are all trying to catch them. But, er …' she tried to smile reassuringly. 'If they come near you, they'll kill you.'

Jasper thumped his head. 'Nice,' he said to Saffy. 'Like that's not going to freak him out.'

But strangely, Boris didn't look scared. His face had taken on a stony expression.

'It's because of the monsterness in your body,' Felix tried to explain. 'Their antennae sense monsters, and … Boris?'

Boris's eyes had glazed over. He wasn't listening.

Jasper took over. 'You need to come back to the school with me. All the Whispered are camping out in a room back at the mansion. The monsters can't get to us there, but they *can* get to us here, so we should probably move. You know, before they sting us to death.'

Boris shook his head, but started towards the mansion. 'No can do. I will escort you back to the mansion. But I will then continue with my guard duty as ordered.'

'*This* is why he's a prefect,' Felix whispered to Jasper. 'He's obsessed with following orders. It's just not *right*.'

Boris was striding towards the school.

But Jasper wasn't giving up that easily. 'Boris! Listen! They'll take back their orders as soon as they know you're a Whispered –'

Boris stopped so suddenly that Jasper smacked painfully into his back. Jasper was really beginning to wonder whether Boris shoved bricks down his top. The prefect turned around and stuck his finger in Jasper's face.

'No!' he said forcefully. 'We don't tell anyone! Anyone! Understood?' Boris's left eye had begun to twitch, and the veins in his forehead were popping out. Jasper heard Felix whimper softly behind him.

'OK, sure,' Jasper said, holding up his hands. 'But please, *please* stay in the school. If they find you, the Skrinkerscreech will kill you!'

Boris shook his head. 'Thanks for trying to protect me. But I promised to do my duty and to obey every order I am given. And that's what I will do. It's what I *have* to do.'

Jasper kicked a mound of snow in frustration. 'But you were only given those orders because no-one knew you'd be in danger! If they knew ...'

But Boris had already started off towards the school again, dragging Jasper behind him.

Felix started after them. 'You tried,' he said to Jasper.

Jasper shook his head. 'Fine,' he fumed. 'If you are that stupid and stubborn, then fine. But I'm going to tell Hermes. And if you get kicked out or whatever, at least you'll be alive.'

'Well, as long as I *am* alive, I'm going to follow my orders,' said Boris, as he broke through the forest and stormed across the snowy plain.

'Hang on!' Saffy called sharply.

Boris stopped and turned around. '*What?*'

Saffy shook her head and moved quietly back to the cover of the trees. Boris followed.

'Something's not right,' Saffy said. 'Listen.'

'All I can hear is the wind,' Felix whispered.

'Exactly,' Saffy replied. 'No noise. No talking, no yelling, no anything. Everyone was supposed to be gathering screechwort and heading back to the assembly hall. The fourth-year crews were going to stand guard outside, but no-one's there. Something's happened. I don't like this. Not one bit.'

Jasper shivered and his eyelids fluttered shut.

COOM ... MING ... KLUSE ... NAAO ... KLUUSSE.

The whispering made Jasper jump. What was it saying? Señor Hermes had taught him how to see the words written down on piece of paper in his head. Jasper concentrated.

COMING CLOSE NOW, CLOSE, he read.

It sounded like a warning. Or was his monster side *excited*? One thing was for sure – the monsters were close. Where were they? He couldn't see anything. But he could *hear* something. A soft, low buzzing.

Jasper's heart pounded in his chest. He held his breath. And then he saw it.

A Skrinkerscreech was coming their way.

105

The Skrinkerscreech looked like an overgrown, mutated insect. It had huge, hideous nippers and a fanged face. Its plate-sized eyes were like a fly's, divided into hundreds of gleaming sections. Twitching antennae poked out the top of its head – but one of these was twisted, as though the monster had been in a fight. Its body had a hard, shiny casing like a beetle's, which curved around to end in a pointed stinger.

The monster slashed at some leaves with its sharp nippers. It paused, then rose into the air, its wings moving in a blur. A long line of screechwort drifted behind as it made a beeline towards the mansion.

Jasper let out his breath. It hadn't seen them or sensed them. Maybe because its antennae was mangled. They had been lucky.

Felix had his eyes clenched shut. 'Has it gone?'

'All clear,' Boris said.

'That isn't supposed to be happening,' Saffy said uncertainly. 'The nest should have been built by now. The plan was that as soon as the swarm entered the assembly hall, everyone would jump out and spray the drones with dog drool.'

'So what is a drone doing gathering screechwort?' Jasper asked.

'Exactly,' Saffy replied grimly. 'Something's gone wrong.'

'At the assembly hall?' Boris checked. Saffy nodded. Boris pulled out a pair of binoculars and held them up. 'Ah. Ah-ha. Mmmmm, that's what happened.'

Saffy, Felix and Jasper waited.

Boris kept watching. 'Ewww,' he winced. 'That's got to be painful.'

'What?' Saffy hissed. 'What is going on?'

Boris let the binoculars drop. 'The students are being held prisoner. By the huge bug-things. The situation does not seem to have gone as planned,' he added, somewhat unnecessarily.

Jasper grabbed the binoculars and peered through the lenses, trying to see into the hall. 'Oh,' he murmured.

Through the window of the hall, Jasper could see students lying in a large heap on the floor. Two of the older students – presumably the ones Saffy said were guarding the doors –

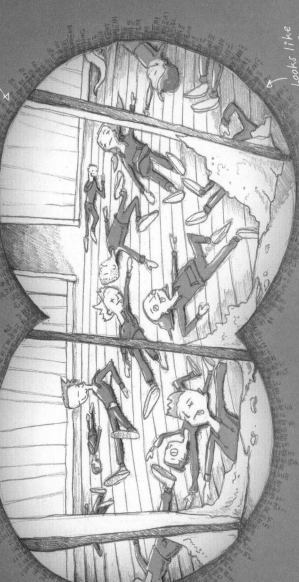

Asleep or dead?

Looks like fumes

View through Boris's binoculars

had broken out in blistering hives. It was truly disgusting.

'By the look of it, most people have fainted,' Jasper relayed.

'They might be paralysed. The drones will be releasing their fumes,' Felix said thoughtfully.

Jasper put the binoculars down and turned to Felix. 'Huh? What fumes?'

'When the queen is ready to lay her eggs, the drones let off fumes,' explained Felix. 'You know how Stenka said when people are attacked, their burst hives release a fear gas? It's the same kind of gas. It paralyses anything in the vicinity. It's to protect the queen.'

Saffy grabbed the binoculars. 'They've taken over,' she muttered. 'We're completely outnumbered. And even if we weren't, it looks like the monsters saw right through our plan anyway.'

'We'll have to get the teachers,' Felix replied. 'It's the only way. We can't do anything on our own.' He turned to Boris. 'Stenka said they'd communicate with the prefects in case of an emergency. Have you got your radio?'

Boris pulled out his radio, and pressed the button on the side.

Eeeoorryyyyyeeeeeccckk! A high-pitched squeal came from the radio.

'There's interference from something!' said Boris.

'Maybe it's these,' said Saffy, pulling out her tin can walkie-talkie out of her pocket.

'Can't you turn them off?' asked Boris, exasperated.

'They are off.' Saffy flicked the switch at the bottom of the walkie-talkies. The feedback became louder and more high-pitched.

Boris moved his radio closer to the walkie-talkies. There was a bright spark of light and a loud bang.

'Ow!' yelped Boris, dropping his radio into the snow. It sizzled and let off steam.

'Well, you can't expect them to be perfect,' huffed Saffy.

At least the squealing had stopped.

Jasper turned to Felix. 'Could we just wait it out? I mean, after the Skrinkerscreech have hatched and fed on the screechwort, they'll leave, right?'

'Who knows?' said Felix. 'I learnt in my lesson with Stenka that they always lay twenty-three eggs. So there will be twenty-three new monsters that have just hatched, plus the original nineteen monsters. And heaps of food for the hatchlings. They might decide they like it here – especially once they've killed off any other monsters in the area.'

Jasper gulped. 'We've got to do something.'

'What does the queen look like?' asked Saffy.

'Oh, you know,' said Felix. 'Enormous mutant insect. Freaky eyeballs, nippers that could cut you in half. Like the other one we saw – but bigger. If she hasn't laid yet, she'll have an abdomen full of monster eggs. And she doesn't have a stinger, so she'll be surrounded by drones to protect her.'

Saffy handed Jasper the binoculars. 'I can't see her, can you?'

Jasper checked out the scene. Saffy was right. The queen was missing. 'Maybe the monsters didn't use your nest, Saff. Maybe they made another one.'

'No way,' Saffy scowled. 'It was perfect.'

Boris was pacing up and down in the snow. 'Do I protect the students? Or do I deliver them as ordered?' he muttered to himself. 'They are

113

both orders. But which one is the overriding order? Which one do I follow?' His eyes were darting all over the place. 'I can't ask my superior, because he doesn't know about monsters ... and ... and –'

'The first thing we need to do is get you two back to safety,' Felix interrupted. 'Saffy and I can handle the rest, but you two could get *killed*, so come on. MOVE IT!' he barked.

Jasper had never seen Felix so serious. He suspected any argument from him would just get him karate kicked, so he nodded.

Felix's outburst seemed to convince Boris that, for now, the most important matter was survival. 'Keep low, and move slowly,' Boris whispered. 'The enemy will be intent on gathering supplies for their nest. They think they have the whole army captive, so they won't be expecting an ambush.'

'There are too many of them,' said Felix. 'We need a better plan.'

'You're right, Felix,' Saffy said. 'Let's go to the Reversal Room. That's the safest place. And it's where the teachers are.' She paused. 'Um, does anyone know where the Reversal Room actually is?'

Felix and Jasper shrugged.

'Not really,' said Jasper. 'But I think I know how we can get back into the school. Come on.'

They came to a stop outside the door Jasper had used before. It would take them through the tunnel and back to the bathroom.

'I thought I was the only one who knew about this tunnel,' said Saffy as she climbed through the door into the tunnel beyond.

Typical, thought Jasper. But he had to smile. Saffy made it her business to know every exit in the school.

Boris just managed to squeeze himself inside the tunnel. Then Felix and Jasper climbed in behind him, and closed the door.

'Are you sure about this?' Felix asked as they crawled along the tunnel.

'What else can we do?' said Jasper. 'Anyway, if we get attacked, I'm the one who is facing a painful death. All you have to worry about is being covered in hives and looking like a hideous freak.'

They followed the tunnel for ten minutes until they reached the air vent above the bathroom. One by one, they dropped down to the floor below.

Felix took his asthma puffer out of his back pocket and breathed deeply. 'Thank goodness that's over. Tunnels are creepy.'

There was a muffled scream in the corridor outside the bathroom.

'But probably not as creepy as whatever's on the other side of that door,' said Jasper.

'Let's check it out,' said Boris.

Felix pocketed his puffer and grabbed a spare flask of dog drool from his hunt belt. He pressed it into Boris's hands. 'You might need this,' he said. 'Even you couldn't squash these insects.'

Boris kicked open the door, his dog drool at the ready. Directly outside the bathroom was a ring of drones. They didn't even look up as the door flew off its hinges. Their stingers were pointed at a slumped figure lying in the middle of the circle, and they were intently wiggling closer and closer.

Jasper gasped. 'Matheson!' he screamed. The drone in front of Jasper looked up, its antennae twitching and its nippers slicing the air. But it kept its stinger trained on Matheson.

'RUN!' Felix commanded Jasper.

But there was no way Jasper was backing out of this. If it wasn't for him, Matheson would be tucked up safely in the Reversal Room with all the other Whispered kids.

Why didn't he go back when he saw I'd escaped? Jasper thought.

But he knew already. When Woof raised the alarm, Matheson probably went through the door on the other side of the bathroom trying to save Jasper, and he didn't make it back to safety himself. There was no way Jasper was letting Matheson get stung to death now.

Jasper gave an almighty yell and charged forwards. He was pulled back by Boris, who flung Jasper towards Felix and Saffy. Meanwhile, Boris leapt skywards and sprayed a long arch of dog drool over the drones.

Boris's spray hit half of the monsters

full-on. They stumbled around, then froze solid. The other drones appeared to be in some sort of killing trance, ignoring everything but Matheson.

Jasper shook his flask and flung drool over the closest drone. Felix and Saffy threw drool over the other three drones, as Jasper pulled Matheson out of the way.

There was silence. All the drones were frozen.

Saffy checked Matheson over. 'He seems OK. Just … unconscious,' she reported.

Felix pulled out his asthma puffer and inhaled deeply. 'That,' he wheezed, 'was,' he took another deep puff, 'close.'

'Eight down. How many of these things are there, anyway?' Boris asked, inspecting a frozen drone.

'Er, eighteen. And the queen,' Jasper replied.

120

DRONES!

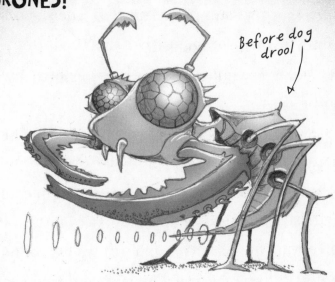

Before dog
drool

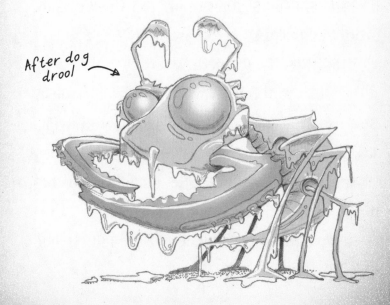

After dog
drool

'Great! Eleven more! Well, what are we waiting for?' Boris nodded.

'I take it you're feeling the buzz, then?' Jasper asked.

'Wooohooo!' Boris replied, jumping in the air.

'No, no, no, no, no,' Felix said. 'We need a plan! A really good one! We don't even know where the queen is. We can't just waltz around and start spraying! And anyway, we need to go past the Species Studies room. I'm almost out of drool.' Felix shook his near-empty flask.

'Got it!' Saffy beamed.

'Is this another plan like the big nest? Because that one didn't turn out too well,' Jasper pointed out.

Saffy glared at him. 'The assembly hall has heaps of fearful vibes, right?' she said.

Jasper and Felix nodded. After all, it had

been the place where everyone was told about the monsters.

'But there's somewhere in the school even more terrifying. I can't believe I didn't think of this before! Think about it. Somewhere we all dread. A place we all have to confront our fears.'

'The Trail of Terror!' Felix and Jasper replied. 'Of course!'

'*That* is where the queen will be, and *that* is where we'll have to go,' Saffy said triumphantly.

'But what about the Skrinkerscreech?' Felix whispered. 'They'll sense Jasper and Boris in a second.'

'Exactly,' Saffy smiled.

Jasper looked at her. 'Look, I know I can be annoying, but killing me? Don't you think that's going a tad too far?'

Saffy looked thoughtful. 'Hopefully it won't get to the killing bit. But we *do* want the monsters to sense you. Felix, how many drones stay with the queen during nesting?' she asked.

'Five, I think,' Felix replied.

'OK, so here's the plan. We need to tempt those five drones away from the nest. We can't get to the nest with them in the room, otherwise they'll just gas us like the others, yeah?'

Felix and Jasper nodded, and Boris grinned even wider. He was getting the hang of the whole Hunt thing.

'So what will tempt the drones out?' Saffy prompted.

'The threat of another monster,' said Jasper. 'Me.'

'Or *us*,' Boris added, thumping Jasper on the back and almost sending him flying across the hallway.

Felix was groaning softly to himself.

'The Trail of Terror has a corridor leading off it,' Saffy continued. 'We'll wait just around the corner. As long as you can outrun them to the end of the corridor, we'll have you covered.'

Boris nodded enthusiastically. 'Yeah, no worries. Right on!'

'So,' said Saffy, 'all we need to do now is get some more drool, and … '

Suddenly a pair of prefects appeared, completely oblivious to the frozen monsters nearby. 'ON THE GROUND! NOW!' yelled one of them, and barrelled Saffy to the floor.

'Wait! I have a cancel card!' said Saffy.

'Him! It's him we want,' said the other prefect, pointing his baton at Jasper.

'Hang on!' Boris boomed. 'I have this under control. He's under prefect arrest.' He nodded towards Jasper.

'Under arrest? Why isn't he restrained then?' asked first prefect, who still had Saffy pinned.

Boris smiled. 'Tactics. I was treating them nice until I had backup, just in case they tried something.' He looked the other prefects up and down. 'But now that you're here, I don't think I need it anyway. These three are a piece of cake. And unless you'd like to take it up with me personally,' he added with a sneer, 'you're not taking any of my prefect points for bringing them in.'

The prefects were both smaller than Boris. The one on top of Saffy stood up slowly. 'Yeah, whatever,' he said. 'Just because your brother got the most prefect points last year …' But they backed away and slunk off down the corridor.

Jasper, Saffy and Felix turned to Boris, whose sneer had turned into a grin.

'Prefect points?' Felix asked.

'Don't you know? The more penalty points we give you, the more prefect points we earn. That's why the prefects are always trying to nab you lot,' Boris explained.

Jasper was secretly impressed. Boris hadn't only disobeyed orders, but he'd lied to the other prefects to save them.

Saffy beamed. 'We just might make a monster-hunter out of you after all.'

The Trail of Terror lay just ahead. Jasper could see the door. He knew that inside, they'd not only find their greatest fears, but possibly also a whole bunch of monsters that wanted to kill him. He took long, deep breaths, psyching himself up to be bait.

'Come on,' Boris moaned. 'You're taking so long!'

Jasper looked at Felix. 'I think I liked him better in prefect mode,' he muttered. 'And Saffy, the dog drool you put all over me has dried now, so it won't be any use. But I'm very sticky and stink like a dog. Thanks a lot,' Jasper finished.

Saffy had decided to cover Boris and Jasper in dog drool in case the monsters ran them down. 'Better safe than sorry,' she said curtly.

They had collected as many flasks of dog drool as they could carry from the Species Studies classroom. Saffy and Felix had flasks all around them. *If* Jasper and Boris could make it to the end of the corridor, they'd be fine.

'Remember,' Felix said, 'if you can hear the buzzing, then it's probably too late. You'll have to tempt the drones out without leaving it for too long. Can you do that?'

'I think so.' Jasper looked at Boris. He was a bit worried that Boris's monster side would get the better of him and he'd completely freak out. Jasper at least had some practice in controlling his whispering, but Boris didn't. There was a good chance his whispering would lead him straight into the path of the monsters. 'If you hear me say run, then run.'

Boris smiled. 'No worries.'

'Break a leg,' Saffy said, shoving Jasper down the hallway.

Jasper and Boris jogged down the corridor. They had no idea how close they had to be for the monsters' antennae to sense them. Jasper hoped the plan worked. Otherwise, they were total goners.

They stopped at the door to the Trail of Terror. A sign on the door read, 'Do not enter. Class 2B test.'

Jasper crouched, ready to run at the slightest sign.

He closed his eyes and listened. At first there was nothing. But then the whisper started racing through his head. The words were so quick that Jasper couldn't catch them. Jasper tried to stay calm as they became louder and louder. He pictured a blank piece of paper in his mind and tried to see the words on it.

KLUUSS ... NAAOOO. KLUUSS ... NAAOOO. NAAOOOO. NAO!

Close now! Jasper jumped up. 'RUN!' he yelled, dragging Boris to his feet. Jasper couldn't hear any buzzing, but he knew it wouldn't take long. They raced down the hallway. A bang from behind made Jasper glance over his shoulder. The drones had burst through the door.

Then Jasper heard the buzzing. *Four seconds.* They were almost at the end of the corridor. Jasper could feel the wind from the drones' wings as they sped towards him. He got to the corner and dived around it. Boris flew on top of Jasper, knocking the wind out of him.

From underneath Boris, Jasper saw the drones freeze mid-flight and collapse on the ground.

There was muffled cheering and Boris clambered off Jasper, who tried to suck some air into his lungs. If Boris had stayed on top of him for much longer, Jasper was sure he would have suffocated.

'One, two, three, four, five!' Felix crowed as he counted the frozen drones.

'That was awesome!' Saffy exclaimed. 'This dog drool stuff is great. If only all monsters had this as their weakness, Hunts would be a cinch!'

'Easy for you to say,' Jasper wheezed. 'You just have to spray 'em.'

'Not quite,' Saffy replied. 'That was the easy bit. Now comes the hard part. The Trail of Terror.'

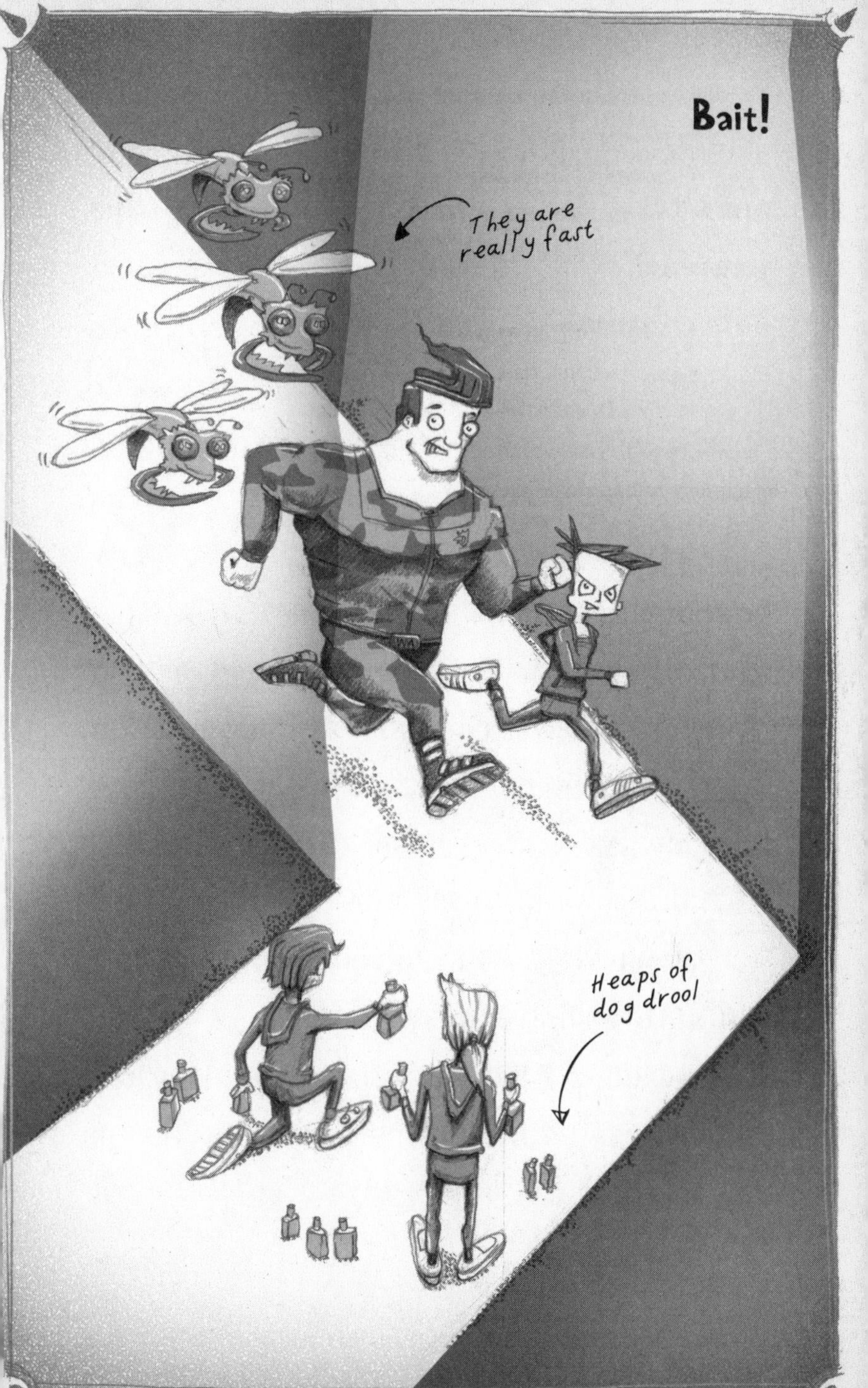

Bait!
They are really fast
Heaps of dog drool

'You should be all right, seeing as you're the one with all the cancel cards. You mustn't have screamed at your worst fear,' Felix pointed out.

'Mmm,' Saffy said airily.

'So, you're *sure* there won't be any more drones?' Jasper said.

Felix shrugged, 'Yeah, I'm sure. Well, pretty sure. At least, I think so.'

'Great, that makes me feel so much better,' Jasper mumbled, checking his flask of dog drool. 'There's not much left. Do you guys have any?'

'Nah, we've just used most of it,' said Felix. 'But don't worry, the queen doesn't have a stinger, so she's harmless.'

'And we've got your back,' said Saffy. 'You'll be fine.'

They walked slowly towards the Trail of

Terror. The door was hanging open, and the path inside was dark and narrow. It twisted around corners, so it was impossible to know what was around the next bend.

Felix started shaking beside Jasper, and Saffy's breathing had become shorter. But there was no choice. They had to find the queen. And she was in there somewhere. She had to be.

'Well, there's only one way to find out,' Jasper muttered, and stepped into the room.

Jasper waited in the darkness. He could hear Saffy, Felix and Boris breathing quietly behind him. The door to the room swung shut with a loud *creeeeaaaak*.

'Please tell me one of you did that,' Saffy whispered.

No-one answered. Jasper knew that the fears of every kid in their class lay inside this room. And a queen Skrinkerscreech with twenty-three eggs, or possibly twenty-three hatchlings feeding on screechwort. Jasper suddenly wondered how long it took the hatchlings to mutate into ferocious, hideous monsters, but he figured it was probably too late to ask Felix.

Footsteps echoed around them, but they couldn't see anyone coming. Suddenly, candles ignited overhead, and a flickering light cast spooky shadows on the walls. The footsteps became louder.

'Well, I'm not just gonna stand here waiting,' Saffy whispered. 'Come on!'

The footsteps were really eerie. Jasper didn't want to see who they belonged to.

They turned a corner and a huge rat came scurrying along the floor, followed by a horde of mice. Jasper saw Felix squirming, but rodents were something they could all handle. The room could get a lot worse.

The footsteps had stopped.

The four kids bunched together, trying not

to bump into anything as they walked.

'We need a new plan,' Felix hissed.

'Isn't it a bit late to be planning now?' Jasper replied. 'I thought the plan was get in, get the eggs, get out. Come on, let's keep moving.'

Around the next corner, Jasper felt something prickle at his neck. He stopped and slowly put his hand up to his shoulder. A huge tarantula crawled onto the back of his fingers. Jasper yelped and flung the spider away. He could see more spiders crawling from the walls, scuttling towards him on their hairy, horrible legs, or spinning down from above.

Felix brushed frantically at Jasper's shoulders and Saffy hurtled any spiders that came too close out of the way. Boris sprayed the others with his dog drool, which worked surprisingly well.

'OK, a new plan would be good,' said Jasper.

Boris was inspecting a bloody sword next to a realistic-looking severed head. 'Cool,' he murmured.

'Mental manipulation,' Saffy said, turning to Jasper. 'What did you learn in your tutorial today? It was some sort of Mental Manipulation, wasn't it? That's what you're good at.'

Jasper thought back to his lesson with Mr Z. It seemed so long ago. 'Nothing of use. I barely had any time,' Jasper answered.

'You must have learnt *something*,' Saffy huffed. '*I* invented a walkie-talkie, Felix learnt everything about the Skrinkerscreech, and you learnt ... what?'

'I didn't really learn anything,' said Jasper. All Mr Z had said was that Jasper had found his tune. Mr Z hadn't taught him how to make people forget. And even if he had, how would that help?

Unless we could forget our fears, Jasper thought uncertainly. *But what if something goes wrong? What if we forget where we're going or what we're doing in here?*

Jasper saw some small, blank faces growing in the walls around them. They looked at Saffy.

'Oh no,' said Saffy. Her face turning pale, she grabbed Jasper's arm. 'Please Jasp, *try*,' she pleaded.

Saffy *never* pleaded.

'*Saffy …*' a voice called softly through the room.

Saffy's eyes grew wide. She grabbed her earplugs and was about to shove them into her ears when Jasper snatched them out of her hands.

'I'll try,' he said and tossed the earplugs to Boris. 'Boris, put these in. Just in case this doesn't work and we end up forgetting why we're here. Whatever happens, lead us to the queen. When we get there, stop me whistling. Got it?'

Boris nodded.

Jasper really hoped this would work. Boris was pretty tough. And besides, the Trail of Terror had been set up for Class 2B. Jasper was betting that if Boris wasn't in their class, his fear wouldn't be in here.

Meanwhile, dolls had started popping out of the walls. They floated through the air towards Saffy. *'Why did you hurt me, Saffy?'* asked a Barbie doll with a melted face in a sing-song voice. The dolls surrounded Saffy and pulled at her hair and clothes. She swatted at them, screaming.

Jasper began whistling the *Sesame Street* song. He wished his tune was something cooler. But he closed his eyes and kept whistling, imagining Mr Z in his beach chair with a drink in his hand.

Saffy stopped screaming and Jasper opened his eyes, still whistling his tune. The dolls were poised in front of her, but Saffy didn't seem so frightened anymore. She looked curiously at the mangled dolls, as though they were an exhibit in a museum.

Boris shoved everyone into a line. 'Link up,' he said. Jasper, Felix and Saffy held hands and followed Boris.

More fears popped out from the walls. Witches' faces, dead people, moths, birds, cockroaches, a rabid-looking monkey, brussels sprouts. But it was more like a being on a ghost train than the Trail of Terror.

Jasper kept whistling. Even when Saffy started laughing at a few of the fears – and really, a pile of cheese *was* a strange fear – he didn't stop. He'd almost forgotten why he was whistling in the first place, but he knew he had to keep on going.

The Trail of Terror

They turned one last corner. Boris removed his earplugs and put his hand over Jasper's mouth.

A lush green screechwort nest rose up in front of them. A soft, gentle humming was coming from deep inside.

A majestic monster was sitting there, on top of twenty-three colourful eggs bundled in the nest.

They had found the queen.

16

'Cripes,' Felix gasped.

Jasper, Saffy and Boris stood with their mouths hanging open. Jasper had never thought he would find a monster beautiful, but the queen was amazing. Her body shimmered, and almost seemed to glow. Her wings whirred softly and she blinked at Jasper with soft, doe-like eyes.

The queen's wings fluttered gently above her eggs, as if she was caressing them.

'The eggs,' said Jasper. But he wasn't sure

anymore why he had wanted them. He was completely mesmerised by the queen.

The queen still hummed softly. She didn't seem to notice them standing in front of her. Jasper sighed, then leapt onto the nest, clambering over the screechwort towards the queen. Jasper listened to the humming. He closed his eyes and felt completely at peace.

She's beautiful, thought Jasper. But something told him this was wasn't quite right.

The whispering burst into his head.

JAAA ... SPEER! DAAN ... GEERR ... USSSS! MON ... STEERSS ... BEWAARE!

Jasper read the words as they scrawled themselves on his mental pad.

Dangerous! Monsters beware!

His eyes flew open. He turned to look at the queen again and screamed.

The dream queen

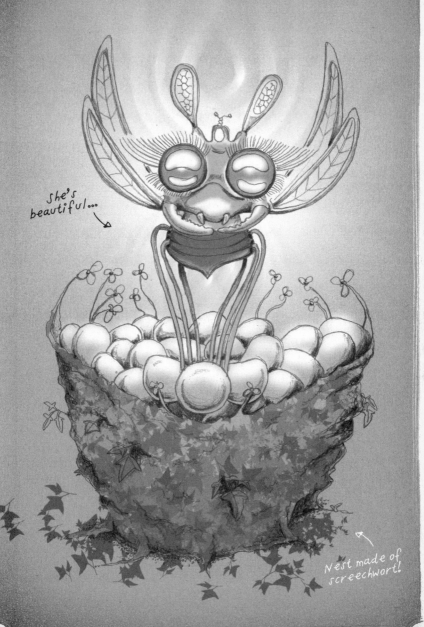

She's beautiful...

Nest made of screechwort!

The queen rose up in her nest. She wasn't beautiful anymore. She was hideous. And absolutely terrifying. Huge, fanged mandibles protruded from her face. Her eyes were red, and her skin rippled with anger.

The queen sprang from the nest. Her gentle humming had turned into a horrible screech.

She flew towards Jasper with such force that he fell back, cracking his head on the floor. He rolled out of the way, just as she pounced down with her nippers gnashing. She might not have had a stinger, but the queen certainly wasn't harmless.

Felix and Saffy were staring at the nest in a kind of awe. Felix was even swaying back and forth. Boris was still looking adoringly at the queen. But the queen was focused on Jasper.

Jasper got gingerly to his feet. 'OK. Definitely *not* beautiful.'

Jasper had a bit of dog drool left in the flask on his belt. He only had one shot at this.

The queen flew up into the air again, shrieking, then darted down towards Jasper. He loosened the flask from his belt and held it behind his back until the very last moment.

When the queen was almost on top of him, Jasper smashed the drool onto her head with all his strength, then dived out of the way.

The queen froze, and fell to the floor with a loud thump.

Jasper let himself breathe again. He was drenched in what he seriously hoped was sweat.

'Wha–?' Felix mumbled, turning towards Jasper.

'What happened?' Saffy asked, rubbing her eyes. 'Where did she go? She was so beautiful ...'

He pointed to the queen.

'Eeew,' Saffy replied. Even Boris shuddered.

'Um, sorry, mate,' Felix added.

'Yeah, good one though,' Saffy grinned.

'No worries, I'll just leave the eggs to you lot,' Jasper replied.

'Oh yeah, the eggs.' Felix looked up at the nest. 'Any ideas?'

But Saffy was already busy tearing down the room's tatty old curtains and pulling it into a makeshift sack for the eggs.

Boris looked into the nest. 'None have been cracked yet. That's good, right?'

'Definitely good,' Felix answered.

Boris carefully handed the eggs down from the nest. 'They're freezing cold!' he said, surprised.

'Yeah, they're monster eggs,' said Felix. 'That's what they're like.'

Together they counted out twenty-three eggs into the sack.

Felix tied a knot tightly around the sack. 'We did it! We actually did it!' he said, clapping his hands.

Jasper slumped to the floor. He felt as if he could sleep for a year. He closed his eyes and sighed happily. *We did it.*

Boris hauled Jasper to his feet. 'No time to rest! We still have five more drones to freeze, and all the students to save, remember? They're either covered in hives or paralysed by fear. Come on, let's get some more dog drool from the Species Studies classroom and freeze the rest of them.' Boris thumped Jasper fondly on the back, as Jasper groaned.

Jasper sat in the food hall, picking at a piece of stale bread. He didn't think he'd ever felt so exhausted. By the time they'd finished freezing the last of the monsters, he could have dropped on the spot. Every muscle in his body ached, and his head throbbed as though someone had whacked him with a cricket bat.

Felix scraped mould off his cheese and Saffy was staring vaguely into space. Only Boris still seemed to have some energy left. He was jigging excitedly up and down in his seat.

The food hall was eerily quiet. Most of the students were recovering in the school hospital, and the teachers were busy airing out the assembly hall and removing the frozen Skrinkerscreech from the hallways.

The only people in the food hall were the Whispered kids, who'd spent the last hour gathered around Felix, Jasper, Saffy and Boris, wanting all the details.

'I can't believe I missed out on the action,' said Mac. 'I wish I'd been there. But listen, Jasper. You'd better watch out for Señor Hermes. You really got him riled by running off like that.'

Jasper buried his head in his hands. Obviously the fact he'd saved the school from monsters hadn't impressed Hermes.

Jasper wasn't sure what he'd say to Señor Hermes. It wouldn't be long before the teachers had finished getting rid of the monsters and seeing to all the other students – and then they would come to the food hall.

'Heads up!' Mac called from the doorway.

Jasper froze. Señor Hermes was storming down the corridor towards the food hall.

'McPhee!' Hermes called out. 'Is McPhee in there?'

Saffy looked at Jasper. 'I would run if I – '

'DOMINGUEZ!' yelled Master Poon, suddenly towering over them in his full camouflage. 'I'm going to give you five seconds to hand back my cancel cards, and then I'll get angry,' Master Poon warned.

Saffy reached into the pocket of her hoodie. 'Here!' she said, handing a pack of cards to Master Poon. Jasper's jaw dropped.

'You mean, you didn't *earn* them? You stole them?' Felix gasped.

'I prefer to think of it as unburdening Master

155

Poon's pocket of his – *awrrfff!*' the rest of Saffy's excuse was muffled as Master Poon lifted her up by her hoodie.

'You could have given us some!' Jasper said.

'McPHEE!' Señor Hermes marched across the food hall, his eyes locked onto Jasper.

I'm never getting out of this one, thought Jasper.

A pack of prefects burst into the food hall. 'Oi! Boris!' one of them snarled. 'We need a word with you. Come outside and have a chat.'

Felix looked from the prefects to Master Poon, to Hermes, and back to the prefects, and started backing away towards the door. 'Maybe I'll just, er … leave, now.'

But his exit was blocked by an old man on horseback.

'Ah, here you are, my young monster-hunters!' Von Strasser's voice rang through the food hall. Everyone turned to face him as he trotted in on his horse.

'Well done, you four. Well done, indeed,' Von Strasser beamed. Jasper sighed in relief. 'You eight-handedly saved the entire school population from the swarm of Skrinkerscreech, *and* prevented the hatchlings from feeding on the screechwort. I am most pleased by your success.'

Jasper glanced quickly at Señor Hermes to check his reaction. Hermes still didn't seem pleased. Jasper decided this was his chance.

'Um, sir, I wondered if we could talk to you about something?' Jasper edged slightly away from Hermes.

Von Strasser looked expectantly at Jasper. 'Why, of course. Ask away, Mr McPhee.'

'Ah, could we talk to you in private?' Jasper said.

'Yes, of course.' Von Strasser appeared to only

just notice that Master Poon had Saffy dangling in the air. 'When Master Poon has finished his demonstration of weightlessness as a relaxation technique,' he added courteously.

Master Poon dropped Saffy and deftly counted his cards. 'Missing three. That's six penalty points you should have had. Another twenty-six should do for taking the cards.'

Saffy nodded meekly.

'And if you ever disobey me again,' Señor Hermes glared at Jasper, 'I'll show you a monster side that's out of control.'

Jasper gulped. 'Yes, sir.'

The circle of prefects had grown tighter like a pack of hungry wolves. They were waiting for Von Strasser to leave.

'Come, then!' Von Strasser called and clicked his horse forward.

'Can Boris come too?' Jasper added quickly.

'Of course,' said Von Strasser.

'It's about Boris,' Jasper began, when they were all outside the food hall, away from the teachers and prefects.

Von Strasser nodded. 'Already done. It's what I came to tell you, in fact,' he winked. 'Welcome to Monstrum House, Boris.' Von Strasser held his arms wide in welcome. 'I have already switched your enrolment details. You've more than proven your ability to think outside the square, and shown that you know when to follow your gut rather than orders. And, of course, your bravery and strength will be useful as a monster-hunter.'

Boris blinked.

'Well?' Saffy asked impatiently. 'Do you want to hunt monsters or not?'

Boris's smile was all the answer they needed.

'Good, good, a new recruit. Excellent. Just what we need. Of course, you should be a year behind these three,' said Von Strasser looking closely at Boris. 'But you seem to have learnt quite a bit already. And I think with some extra tutorials, you'll be able to start as a second-year student, given your age and experience.'

Boris grinned even wider. 'That would be awesome, sir.'

Jasper thumped Boris on the back. Felix hugged him, and Saffy grinned.

It was going to be a great year at Monstrum House.

Monstrum House

Home sweet home